Over the Crescent Moon

B

A BADGER BLISS BOOK

By

Karen D. Badger

Karen D. Badger

DEDICATION

The Hawai'ian people believe in the concept of three souls...the lower soul (*unihipili*), associated with the physical body, a middle soul (*uhane*), associated with the mental or conscious mind, and a higher soul (*aumakua*), which represents a personal, supernatural higher self, or oversoul. The oversoul is the ultimate source of who and what we are. It follows us through each new life cycle. It contains our essence and all of the experiences we have garnered in our past lives. It is what makes us easily recognizable to each other through all our lifetimes.

I dedicate this book to my older brother Steven Michael Dusablon who left us just short of his 58th birthday. Steve, may our oversouls exchange '*ha*', the divine breath of life, over and over again through all eternity. I miss you like crazy, Bro...and I love you to the [crescent] moon and back.

ALSO WRITTEN BY KAREN D. BADGER AND
AVAILABLE FROM BADGER BLISS BOOKS:

ON A WING AND A PRAYER
YESTERDAY ONCE MORE
THE BLUE FEATHER
ALL MY TOMORROWS
1140 RUE ROYALE
OVER THE CRESCENT MOON

The Billie/Cat Commitment Series:
  IN A FAMILY WAY
  UNCHAINED MEMORIES
  HAPPY CAMPERS
  COLLECTIVE IDENTITY
  SWEET ANGEL
  RELATIVE-LY SPEAKING
  TAILSPIN
  FLASHPOINT

www.badgerblissbooks.com

Over the Crescent Moon

$\mathcal{B}$

A BADGER BLISS BOOK

By

Karen D. Badger

This is a work of fiction. All characters, locales, and events are either products of the author's imagination or are used fictitiously.

OVER THE CRESCENT MOON

Copyright © 2019 by Karen D. Badger
www.karendbadger.com

Cover image: Youssef Jheir (obtained with attribution from Pixabay)
Cover design by Karen D. Badger

A Badger Bliss Book
Published by Badger Bliss Books
Georgia, VT 05468

www.badgerblissbooks.com

Print book ISBN 13: 978-1-945761-26-3
Print Book ISBN 10: 1-945761-26-1
Ebook ISBN 13: 978-1-945761-27-0
Ebook ISBN 10: 1-945761-27-X

First Edition, June, 2019

Printed in the United States of America and in the United Kingdom

Karen D. Badger

ACKNOWLEDGMENTS

In every book I write, I thank those who worked to find my typo's and fix my literary errors. A mere thank you is not enough to acknowledge the contribution of these wonderful women. They truly save me from looking like a total idiot! I hope to be able to work with them for many years to come.

In no special order, they are: Ellie Atherton (my mom and number one fan), 'Chief Eagle Eye' Carol Poynor (soul sister extraordinaire), and last but not least, Barb Sawyer, aka, 'Bliss' (my better half and keeper of my *aumakua* soul). A special thank you to Nat Burns (amazing editor and sister from another mother), who worked tirelessly to complete the edits on a very short timeline.

Thank you, ladies! Hugs and love to all!

Note to readers...

A quick tutorial on the Hawai'ian language:

> The letter "e" is pronounced as a short "e"... as in 'hey'
>
> The letter "a" is pronounced as a short "a"... as in 'ah'
>
> The letter "i" is pronounced as a long "e"... as in 'eee'
>
> The letter "u" is pronounced as "ooo" (as in the word 'you'), or sometimes as a "w"
>
> The letter 'w" is sometimes pronounced as a "v"
>
> The apostrophe is considered a letter and it denotes a glottal stop in the word (see example below)

Every letter in an Hawai'ian word is pronounced.

For example:

> The name "Leilani" is pronounced as "Lay-ee-lah-nee"
>
> The name "Makaya" is pronounced as "Mah-kah-yah"
>
> The name "Makenna" is pronounced as "Mah-ke-nah"
>
> O'ahu is pronounced "O-ah-oo"
>
> Kauai is pronounced "Kah-wah-ee"
>
> The word Hawaii can be pronounced as "Ha-wa-ee" or "Ha-va-ee"
>
> "Ka'anapali" is pronounced "Kah(pause)ah-nah-pah-lee." The apostrophe between the two letters 'a' creates a pause between "kah" and "ah."

Karen D. Badger

Chapter 1

"Spencer, it's time to get up."

"No!" Spencer grabbed the edge of the sheet and pulled it over her head.

"Don't make me break out the claw."

"Just a few more minutes," Spencer whined.

"I'm warning you!"

Spencer peeked out from under the covers. "You don't scare me."

"You asked for it. The claw!"

Spencer threw back the sheet, grabbed her assailant around the waist and slammed her onto the bed. She then sat on top of her and pinned her arms to the bed by her wrists. She leaned in so close, her nose nearly touched that of the person trapped beneath her.

"Nice try, Makaya. You should know better than to threaten me with the claw. So now it's *you* who will pay!" Spencer formed both her hands into claws and unmercifully tickled Makaya as she squirmed and squealed beneath her.

"No! Stop! Okay. Enough! You win." Makaya said as she tried to get away.

Makaya managed to free one leg and flip Spencer onto her back. She took advantage of her sudden freedom to scurry off the bed. She grabbed a pillow and beat Spencer with it. "You little shit!"

Spencer grabbed the other pillow and fought back. "If you play with fire, sooner or later, you'll get burned," she said.

After a few more swipes, Spencer grabbed Makaya's pillow and yanked her down onto the bed. She landed with a thud on her back. In seconds, Spencer was on top of her and once again face to face.

Makaya panted heavily as she stared into Spencer's eyes. "You can be so infuriating," she growled.

Spencer narrowed her eyes, but never broke eye contact. "It's what you love about me most. Don't deny it."

"And you're cocky, too," Makaya added.

"I'll show you cocky."

Spencer slipped one hand under Makaya's neck and tilted her chin upward, placing feather-light kisses on the corners of her mouth.

"You're also a tease," Makaya whined.

Spencer devoured Makaya's mouth, forcing her tongue deep inside. A shudder contracted Spencer's abdomen as she felt Makaya press herself against her. She moaned when Makaya dug her nails into her buttocks.

"I want you," Spencer hissed.

"We'll be late for practice, Spence."

"Fuck practice."

***

"Makaya, Spencer, on your starting marks," the coach called from outside the sparring area.

Both women struck their starting pose and waited for the buzzer signaling the start of the match. When it came, Makaya immediately attacked, extending her arm and continually threatening Spencer's target areas.

Spencer counterattacked by quickly moving back out of the way. She evaded Makaya's aggression by turning to the side and grazing her blade to effectively deflect it so that it missed its mark. She followed the defensive move with a lunge and thrust as she extended her front leg with a slight kicking motion and propelled her body forward with her back leg.

Makaya executed a parry and blocked Spencer's weapon and then followed the move with a riposte attack. Once again, Spencer successfully deflected the counterattack with circle parries and was able to catch Makaya's tip and deflect it away.

"No...no...no! Stop!" The coach ran his hands through his hair and then put them on his hips. Makaya and Spencer stopped and removed their helmets. Spencer frowned impatiently and waited for him to speak.

"Come on, ladies. If you want to be taken seriously as fencers, you need to be more aggressive. You are my top two students. You should be going after one another like you mean it. Now put your helmets back on and show me what you're made of."

Spencer looked at Makaya. "He can be a real asshole." She shoved her helmet back on and went to her end of the sparring area.

"All right then. On your marks!"

As soon as the buzzer sounded, Spencer aggressively executed a beat attack and disturbed Makaya's aim. This allowed her to successfully hit Makaya's arm and draw a high outside parry. She effectively scored first blood.

"That's more like it!" the coach yelled.

Makaya tore her helmet off and glared at Spencer. A hint of mirth filled her eyes and a thin smile formed on her lips. Spencer cocked an eyebrow and grinned.

The coach was immediately on her case. "Put the helmet back on, Makaya. If you do that in a match, you will be disqualified."

With both fencers on their marks, the buzzer sounded the start of the next round.

Makaya tore out of her starting mark and executed two feints, followed by a continuous barrage of attacks. She targeted Spencer's high line above her bell guard and then followed it with a low line attack. She pivoted her blade under Spencer's weapon and tipped her target, scoring a point of her own.

"All right ladies, next point wins. On your marks!" the coach shouted.

Spence came off her mark with a thrust attack and extended her arm to continuously threaten Makaya's mark. Makaya countered with a point-in-line position to disturb Spencer's aim. After several parries and ripostes, Makaya flicked her blade and caused it to bend such that she was able to score a point against the back of Spencer's shoulder.

Spencer tore off her helmet and threw it on the floor. She screamed in frustration.

"Great job, Makaya. You too, Spencer. I have a good feeling about you two. You'll be a force to reckon with in the next competition. That's enough for today. You can hit the showers," the coach instructed.

Spencer watched the coach walk away and then turned to Makaya. "That was dirty pool," she said.

"No—that was a legal move. Spence, you let your anger get the best of you. Hot heads don't win matches. Calm execution does."

Spencer stood with her hands on her hips. Her gaze was directed to the floor.

Makaya rubbed Spencer's arm. "How about that shower? I'll wash your back for you."

Spencer grinned and shook her head. "Why can't I stay mad at you?" she asked.

"Because you can't resist my beauty and charm." Makaya picked Spencer's helmet up and handed it to her. "Here. Let's go get naked."

***

Spencer leaned against the locker room wall and watched Makaya disrobe and walk into the shower. She couldn't get enough of Makaya Kapule's beauty. Her long dark hair and Pacific Islander features turned Spencer's insides to mush every time she walked into the room. Her native Hawai'ian heritage was displayed proudly in her demeanor and in the way she interacted with people. Spencer had fallen hard for her the moment they'd met more than a year ago. She thanked the gods every day for her decision to join the fencing team. She would have never met Makaya otherwise.

Spencer Bennet was aware of how stark the differences were between herself and Makaya. Where Makaya was dark skinned with long black hair and brown eyes, Spencer wore the mantle of her Irish heritage, with fair skin, green eyes and asymmetrically boy-cut auburn hair. Makaya was curvy, with full breasts and hips, while Spencer was pretty much straight up and down. In fact, she'd been called 'sir' may times in her adult life. The only thing they had in common were their ages. They were both in their early thirties and were literally born just a few days apart, but on completely different sides of the world…she, in Vermont and Makaya, in Hawai'i.

Spencer was deep in thought when a wet washcloth hit her on the side of the head.

"Hey! What was that for?" Spencer protested.

Only Makaya's face appeared from behind the shower curtain. She then threw the curtain open and exposed herself in all her glory. "I can't wash your back if you're out there—and still dressed, I might point out. Now get in here…preferably naked."

A grin split Spencer's face as she tore off the remainder of her clothing and joined Makaya in the shower. She pulled the curtain closed behind her and backed Makaya against the side of the shower stall. The high-pressure spray pummeled her back. She placed one hand against the wall on each side of Makaya's head and kissed her passionately.

Spencer's mouth moved to Makaya's neck, exposing Makaya to the spray of water. "Damn, what you do to me," Spencer said.

Makaya's eyes were closed and her head was turned to the right to give Spencer better access to her neck.

Spencer moved on to nibble at Makaya's left shoulder and then with her tongue, she traced the crescent moon tattoo placed strategically above Makaya's breast, with a sprinkle of stars trailing down to her nipple.

"What is this thing you have with my tattoo?" Makaya asked softly, eyes still closed.

"It's sexy," Spencer said. "I am over the crescent moon in love with you."

"You are so corny!"

"I can't help it. You have me under a spell. I turn into a lovesick dork when I'm around you."

Spencer was indeed fascinated with the tattoo. For Makaya, the moon was a symbol of regeneration, and represented a woman's ability to bring life into the world. The moon conveyed secret powers and wisdom...energy and light.

Upon reaching the end of the trail of stars, Spencer inhaled Makaya's nipple into her mouth and pinched it gently between her teeth.

Spencer felt herself being pulled further into Makaya's embrace.

"I need more," Makaya whispered into Spencer's ear.

Spencer reached for the soap and lathered her hands, then slipped one hand in between Makaya's legs. Makaya pressed the back of her head into the shower stall. "Oh, my God, Spence," she moaned.

"You like that, huh?" Spencer watched Makaya's face as she slipped three fingers inside. The desire on Makaya's face drove her close to her own release. An intense heat built in her abdomen and she felt herself shudder. The hot spray of water on her back only intensified the feeling. She struggled to control herself as she focused on Makaya.

Makaya matched Spencer's thrusts and Spencer felt her lover's muscles tighten against her fingers. She knew it wouldn't be long before Makaya went over the edge as well, and the closer she got, the harder it was to control her own climax.

"Mak...Mak, touch me. Please. I don't think I can hold it back," Spencer rasped into Makaya's ear.

Makaya's eyes flew open and she stared directly at Spencer at the same time she slipped two fingers into Spencer's folds.

The sultry look in Makaya's eyes, combined with the caress of her fingers, drove Spencer to orgasm at the same time Makaya reached climax. Spencer leaned against Makaya. It took all her might to hold them both upright as their bodies succumbed. Her weight alone held them up on shaky legs.

Spencer leaned her forehead on Makaya's shoulder. "Damn, woman. I have never felt like this for anyone in my entire life. I love you, Mak."

"I love you too, Spence."

Spencer's head snapped up as she heard the door to the shower room close. She looked at Makaya and grinned. "I wonder how many we've scared away in the last few minutes?"

"Fuck'em if they can't take a joke," Makaya replied.

Chapter 2

Makaya sat on the bleachers and watched Spencer come out of the locker room. A smile crossed her face at the sight of Spencer sauntering across the gym toward her. *Damn, she's sexy,* Makaya thought.

Spencer climbed the few tiers to where Makaya sat and stopped on the step below her.

Makaya leaned forward and accepted a kiss. "How did gymnastics practice go?" she asked.

"Not bad. My floor routine is improving," Spencer said.

Makaya shook her head. "I don't know how you do two sports at once. Fencing takes a lot out of me. I couldn't imagine doing gymnastics on top of it."

Spencer sat down beside her. "I don't think I'm good enough to medal—not to mention, being too old—but it keeps me limber. For me, I feel like it helps me move faster during fencing matches."

"More power to you," Makaya replied.

"How was work today?" Spencer asked.

"It was okay. We had a preemie born today that had to be confined to the NICU. I think the little sweetheart will make it, but she's going to be a sick little girl for a while."

"I don't know how you do it, Mak. It would break my heart to be a nurse in the pediatric ward. I'm a sucker when it comes to sick kids."

"Some days are harder than others, but overall, I love my job. How was your day?" Makaya asked.

"Busy. We are in the middle of qualifying the new semiconductor inspection tool. As you know, if we miss even one defect, there is a chance a computer chip will fail in the field. The last thing we need is for one of my tools to cause an air traffic control error. So far, things are going great. Everything appears to be meeting spec," Spencer explained.

"You're cute when you talk geek," Makaya teased.

"I'm not a geek…I'm an engineer," Spencer corrected.

"No, you are a geek. Changing the subject! Are you ready to go shopping?"

"Shopping?" Spencer asked.

"Yes. Remember? We need to find formal outfits to wear to my sister's wedding in two weeks."

"Yikes! Is that only two weeks away?"

"Yes, and I'm so looking forward to going home for a while. I haven't been back to Hawai'i in three years."

"I've never been. I'm looking forward to it too," Spencer said.

"You are?" Makaya asked.

"Yes. I'm looking forward to seeing Hawai'i for the first time—but nervous about meeting your family—also for the first time."

"They're going to love you, even though you *are* a *haole*." Makaya chuckled at her joke.

"Ha, ha. Very funny!"

"So, are you ready to go shopping?" Makaya asked.

"If I have to, but I'm not wearing a dress."

"No worries. I bet you look amazing in a suit."

"*That*, I can do, but how do you think your family will deal with it?"

"My family has known where my heart lies since I was a teen. They will expect no less. Don't worry so much. It'll be fine."

"I'm glad the wedding is in October. It will be nice to spend time in warmer weather for a little longer before winter hits us here in Vermont."

"It's always summer in Hawai'i. You'll love it there."

Spencer stood and offered her arm. "Okay, then. Let's go shopping!"

***

Spencer enjoyed looking at the plush green foliage as the plane made its approach toward Lihue International Airport on Kauai. "What town does your family live in?" she asked.

Makaya leaned across Spencer to look out the window. "Princeville. It will be about a forty-five minute drive from the airport."

"We're getting a rental car, right?"

"I'm hoping to get a four-wheel drive vehicle. Maybe even a Jeep. There's a ton of off-road trips we can make on the island," Makaya explained.

"Cool!"

"I'm glad we were both able to get two weeks off from work. You can see the whole island in a week, but to enjoy it, you need to stay longer."

Makaya noticed that Spencer's leg bounced up and down. She placed her hand on Spencer's knee. "You know, you don't have anything to worry about. They're going to love you."

"Am I that transparent?"

"Like glass."

"I can't help it. I don't want anything to come between us, and families have a way of doing that. Know what I mean?"

Makaya moved her hand to the side of Spencer's face. "Nothing is going to come between us. You are stuck with me—you got that? I would be lost without you. I love you, Spence, and nothing is going to separate us. Okay?"

Spencer smiled. "Okay. I'll try to relax."

"Thank you, love. *Aloha*, and welcome to Hawai'i," Makaya said as the wheels touched the runway.

***

"This is freaking amazing!" Spencer hung out the Jeep window and took in the topology of Kauai as Makaya drove. "I've never seen trees shaped that way before. They look like tall bonsai trees. Oh, and wow! Look at that waterfall there!"

Makaya leaned forward to look out the windshield. "It's funny—this just looks like home to me. I guess you don't appreciate what is in front of you every day. It's refreshing to see it through your eyes."

"I read that parts of *Jurassic Park* were filmed here," Spencer said.

"Yes. In fact, scenes from lots of movies were filmed here. If we have time, I'll take you around to see a few of the sites."

"The wedding is just a day away, so we should have two weeks to enjoy the island," Spencer pointed out.

"True, but we'll need to spend time with my family." Makaya saw Spencer wince. "I saw that. Relax. I promise it'll be fine."

"So, besides sight-seeing, what else is there to do on the island?" Spencer asked.

"Are you kidding me? What is there *not* to do? Surfing, hiking, zip-lining, fishing, boating, para-sailing, water skiing…"

"Water skiing? That sounds fun. I've done some of that on Lake Champlain," Spencer said.

Makaya laughed. "Sweetheart, water skiing on a small fresh-water lake is nothing like water skiing in the ocean. My older brother has a motorboat and skis. I'll set it up with him right after the wedding."

"I'm looking forward to it!"

***

"Mama, this is Spencer. Spencer, my mom, Alani."

Spencer shook the older woman's hand. "It's so nice to meet you, Mrs. Kapule."

Alani squeezed Spencer's hand and pulled her close. "Do you love my daughter?" she asked.

Spencer's eyes opened wide and she sent a desperate glance in Makaya's direction. "Ah, as a matter of fact, yes, I do. With all my heart," she replied.

"Then you may call me *Makuahine*," Alani said.

"*Makuahine?*" Spencer asked.

"It means, 'mother'."

Spencer grinned. "*Makuahine*, it is, then."

Alani kissed her on both cheeks and then released her hand.

Makaya took Spencer's hand and led her toward an older gentleman. "And this is my father, Kaapo."

Spencer shook his hand. Like his wife, he held Spencer's hand for an extended period of time.

Kaapo nodded toward his wife and grinned. "Don't let her scare you. Her bark is worse than her bite."

Spencer smiled. "Thank you, sir. It's so nice to meet you."

"This is my brother, Kaarle, my sister-in-law, Nayla, and their children, my niece, Paulapula and nephew, Pace."

Kaarle extended his hand. "Nice to meet you, Spencer. We're looking forward to spending time with you. Anyone who can put up with my sister is okay in my book."

Makaya punched Kaarle in the shoulder. "Shut up! You'll pay for that later."

"Makaya tells me you're a boater," Spencer said.

"Yes. I'd be happy to take you out while you're here. Do you water ski?" Kaarle asked.

"I have, but as Makaya likes to point out, my experience is limited to small lakes. I welcome the challenge of water skiing in the ocean."

"It's a date, then."

"I'm looking forward to it."

"Moving on," Makaya said. "This is my baby sister, and the bride to be, Maarika."

Maarika threw herself into Spencer's arms before she could offer her hand. Spencer glanced over Maarika's shoulder to Makaya and smiled and then wrapped her arms around Maarika's waist for a hug.

Maarika stepped back and grinned. "Hi, Spencer. I'm so glad you and Mak could make it for the wedding. You'll meet Kadir tomorrow. Mama insists that we stay apart for a few days before the ceremony. Some tradition, I guess. Anyway, it would not have been the same without Mak here, so thanks for coming with her."

"I'm happy to be here," Spencer said.

Makaya took Spencer's hand. "Okay, now that you've met everyone, let's get you settled in your room. Grab your bag."

Spencer picked up her bag and allowed Makaya to drag her toward a staircase, out of earshot of her family. "*My* room?" she asked.

"Ah, yeah. I forgot to tell you. Mom has a problem with pre-marital co-habitation."

Spencer stopped short. "She *does* know we live together, right?"

Makaya looked at the floor and remained silent.

"Mak? She knows we live together—right?" Spencer repeated.

"Well…"

"Wait. Are you telling me we need to spend the next two weeks sleeping in separate rooms?"

"As far as Mom is concerned, yes. I'm supposed to be bunking with Maarika tonight. After the wedding, Maarika will be moving to Kadir's house, so that opens her room for me to use solo."

Makaya saw the grimace on Spencer's face. "Don't fret. Maarika and I already have it worked out. I'll make a point of letting mom see me go into Maarika's room and then sneak into your room after they go to bed."

"Your sister has agreed to lie for you?"

"Of course. That's what sisters are for."

"Geez Louise! This is going to be an interesting trip."

Chapter 3

Spencer sat next to Makaya in the first row of reserved seats beside Makaya's parents. She looked around with great interest at the venue.

The wedding was being held on the beach of an upscale Princeville resort. Rows of folding chairs were placed neatly in front of a large circle of flowers on the beach. The same flower decorated an arched trellis that hovered above the circle of flowers in the sand. Leis were draped over the back of each chair.

Makaya slipped her hand into Spencer's as her sister Maarika, and soon to be brother-in-law Kadir, strode slowly toward one another from opposite ends of the beach. Maarika was dressed in a flowing white dress, with a white cord around her waist. A ring of flowers graced her head in place of a traditional veil. Her long black hair hung loosely down her back. Kadir was dressed in white trousers with the cuffs rolled half-way up his calves. He wore a white short-sleeve button-up shirt and a red sash around his waist. Both were barefoot. Once they reached the circle of flowers, Kadir offered his hand to Maarika, and together, they stepped into the circle.

Makaya looked at Spencer and smiled. "She looks beautiful."

Spencer held Makaya's gaze as an intense feeling consumed her. All she wanted was to surround herself in the love she saw in Makaya's eyes and to stay there for all eternity.

Their attention was soon drawn to the minister performing the wedding ceremony.

"Welcome family and friends of Maarika and Kadir. There are leis on the backs of your chairs. Please take a moment to don this symbol of love and respect." The minister waited for his instructions to be carried out before he handed leis to the bride and groom.

"Maarika and Kadir, the lei is an unbroken circle that represents your commitment and love for one another. Like a wedding ring, it is unending, with no beginning and no end. Each flower is beautiful on its own, but when it becomes part of the lei, its beauty is enhanced and becomes stronger because of the bond—just as the two of you will become stronger through the bond of marriage. You may now share your lei with your beloved."

The minister turned to all in attendance. "*Aloha* to Maarika and Kadir...and to all our guests. As you know, *Aloha* means both hello and goodbye. With respect to this joyous occasion, we are saying goodbye to the single life and hello to married life for Maarika and Kadir.

"In ancient Hawai'i, when a man was interested in courting a woman, he would approach her with a flower. If she accepted the flower and put it on her left ear, it would mean that she was already spoken for; however, if she put it over her right ear, it was a clear message that she was still available, and interested in a relationship."

The minister retrieved a large flower from the small table beside him and offered it to Kadir. Kadir smiled broadly at Maarika and handed the flower to her. Maarika grinned mischievously and started to place the flower on her left ear. "Just kidding!" she said, and then placed it on her right ear.

The audience laughed and clapped loudly.

"Phew! That was a close one," the minister said. "*Aloha,* Maarika and Kadir!"

Makaya leaned in to whisper in Spencer's ear. "She's such a scamp! I'm not surprised she'd pull something like that."

"I think it's sweet," Spencer said. "She reminds me of someone else I know."

Their attention was soon drawn back to the minister.

"It is now time to exchange rings." The minister retrieved a small bowl made of dark wood, from the table beside him and walked to the ocean's edge to fill it with saltwater. He carried it back to the congregation and then dropped a leaf into the water in the bowl. "Koa is a valuable hardwood that represents strength and integrity, which are two of the fundamental foundations of a good marriage. The Ti leaf represents prosperity, health and blessings for the body, mind and spirit."

The minister placed the bride's ring in Kadir's hand and the groom's ring in Maarika's hand and then proceeded to sprinkle the water on the rings three times. "This water washes away any hindrance to your marriage. It also represents a brand new beginning for you as husband and wife." The minister then held his hands over the rings and chanted, "*Ei-Ah Eha-No. Ka Malohia Oh-Na-Lani. Mea A-Ku A-Pau.* May peace from above rest upon you and remain with you now and forever." He turned to the bride and groom. "You may now exchange rings."

Spencer glanced at Makaya as Maarika and Kadir exchanged rings, and noticed a small tear escape the corner of her eye. A magical look of love and bliss for her baby sister was clearly evident on her face. Again, intense emotion overcame Spencer and she had to fight back tears of her own.

Suddenly, a gentle gust of wind ruffled Spencer's hair. When she looked at Makaya again, there were tears openly flowing down her face.

"Makaya?" Spencer asked.

"They're here," Makaya whispered.

"They're here? Who's here?"

"The *Ohana*. The ancestral family. They have arrived on the wind to give their blessing and support."

The minister once again took center stage. "Family and friends, I give you Maarika and Kadir. Joined as one in love. *Aloha*, one and all."

The congregation erupted in applause and guests and family greeted the newlyweds with warm hugs and well wishes, after which, Spencer, Makaya and Makaya's parents stood aside and waited for the greetings to finish before heading to the reception. Spencer found herself feeling a bit overwhelmed by the event.

"What an amazing ceremony. We should come back here for our wedding," Spencer said.

Makaya cocked her head and raised her eyebrows in surprise. "Spencer Bennet! Did you just propose to me?"

A momentary rush of panic filled Spencer's mind as she realized she did indeed just propose. Funny thing was…she liked the idea. "Ah, I guess I did."

Makaya continued to stare at Spencer with a look of incredulity on her face.

Alani elbowed Makaya in the ribs.

"Ow, Mom! What was that for?"

"*Makemake au i kēia. Mai kuhi oe i ka naaupo. E haʻi aku iā ia.*"

"What did she say?" Spencer asked.

Makaya laughed. "She said she likes you. She also said I would be a fool if I didn't say yes."

Spencer grinned at Alani and then turned her attention back to Makaya. "Do you always do what your mother says?"

"I do when her advice is good."

"And is her advice good this time?"

"Her advice is *very* good this time."

Spencer reached forward and plucked a flower from Makaya's lei and handed it to her. "So, you'll marry me?"

Makaya looked at the flower in her hand for several moments without speaking.

Alani elbowed Makaya in the ribs once more.

"Again, Mom? Okay…okay!" Makaya looked at Spencer and then slowly placed the flower on her right ear. "Yes, I will marry you."

Spencer opened her arms and wrapped them around Makaya. "Thank you, love."

"*E hoʻomaikaʻi iā Pele! I kēia manawa, ʻaʻohe pono ʻoe e komo i loko o ka lumi o Spencer i ka pō. Loaʻa iaʻu kuʻu ʻae,*" Alani said, and then walked away toward the reception.

"Oh, my God, Mom!" Makaya exclaimed. She covered her face with both hands to hide the red hue rapidly growing there.

Spencer held Makaya at arm's length. "What did she say?"

"She said—and I quote—'Praise Pele! Now that it's official, you don't have to sneak into Spencer's room at night. You have my permission.'"

Spencer looked at the retreating back of her future mother-in-law. "Praise Pele, indeed!"

Chapter 4

Makaya stood in the back of the boat and leaned across the motor. "Are you sure you want to do this, Spencer? This isn't Lake Champlain, you know," she called out.

Spencer held the handle of the towrope firmly in her hands. She bobbed up and down in the water behind Kaarle's boat, keeping the tips of her skis above the water, with the towrope between them. Whitecap waves struck her in the face repeatedly.

"Don't baby her, Mak," Kaarle said. He moved the boat slowly forward to take the slack out of the rope. "She's a big girl. She's wearing her lifejacket and goggles. She'll be fine once she's out of the water and on the skis."

"Kaarle, you don't understand. Lake Champlain is a relatively small freshwater lake. These whitecaps are at least five times higher than what's she's used to."

"You and I both know the hardest part is getting up on the skis. After that, she won't even notice the whitecaps."

"But she's already failed to get up twice…and the second fall was a pretty nasty face-plant. I don't need my fiancé getting killed before we're even married."

"Okay, that should just about do it." Kaarle looked over his shoulder at Spencer in the water. "Okay, Spencer, this time, bend your knees and sit back on the skis. As you come out of the water, keep your knees bent, and lean back."

Spencer gave a thumbs-up.

"Here we go!" Kaarle accelerated steadily as Makaya kept her gaze fixed on Spencer who rose smoothly out of the water.

"She's up!" Makaya shouted above the sound of the motor. "Keep it steady Kaarle…and no sharp turns, okay?"

"Yeah, yeah, yeah. She'll be fine, Mak."

Makaya's gaze never left her partner as Spencer weaved back and forth across the wake of the boat. The longer Spencer stayed upright, and the more comfortable she appeared to be. Makaya relaxed. "She seems to be doing okay, Kaarle."

"I knew she would," Kaarle replied. "The whitecaps may be higher on the ocean, but the basics of water skiing are the same, regardless of the body of water you're skiing on. I'm going to try a soft turn. Keep an eye on her."

Makaya motioned to Spencer that there was a turn coming up and then watched carefully as the angle between Spencer and the boat became sharper. At one point it appeared as though Spencer was skiing beside the boat rather than behind it. But still, she remained upright on the skis.

"How's she doing Mak?" Kaarle asked as he steered the boat gracefully through the curve.

Makaya turned to look at her brother. "She's doing fine. You were right, I shouldn't worry so much."

When Makaya turned back around, she screamed, "No! Spencer!"

"What is it?" Kaarle asked.

"Kaarle, stop the boat!   Stop the boat!" Makaya screamed.

Kaarle threw the boat in neutral and then reverse and brought the boat to a halt in the water. A moment later, he stood beside Makaya at the rear of the boat.

"Where is she?" Kaarle asked.

"I...I don't know. She was doing fine. I only looked away for a moment. Spencer!" Makaya screamed her name.

"Where was she when you looked away?"

"Over there."   Makaya pointed into the distance at an angle to the boat.

Kaarle ran to the front of the boat and threw it into gear. "Hold on, we'll go look for her. Pull in the rope."

Makaya pulled the towrope into the boat as Kaarle made his way to the area Spencer was last seen.

"Mak, keep an eye out for the skis. They should be floating on top. That will give us a good idea about where she went down. Damned whitecaps. It's difficult to see anything among them."

"I knew we shouldn't have come out in these waves today. I knew it!" Makaya's voice was panic stricken.

"That's not helping matters, Makaya. Focus. We need to find the skis."

"There! Look there!" Makaya pointed to an object floating on top of the water.

Kaarle turned the boat in the direction Makaya was pointing, and sure enough, they encountered one ski. "Look around, Mak. She's got to be close by," Kaarle said.

"Spencer! Spencer, answer me," Makaya shouted. "I don't see her, Kaarle."

"Keep looking."

Kaarle slowly maneuvered the boat in a circle around where the water ski was found. "She should be here," he said.

"There's the other ski." Makaya once again pointed at an object floating in the water.

They retrieved the second ski and then searched the area between where the two skis were found, to no avail.

Makaya continued to call Spencer's name until her voice was hoarse.

"This doesn't make sense," Kaarle said. She's wearing a life jacket. She should be floating on top."

"We need to call the Coast Guard, Kaarle. We need help." Makaya sank to the floor of the boat and wept. "Spencer. My God. Spencer."

***

Two small boys walked in circles around their discovery on the beach.

"What is this thing?" one of them said.

"'Tis a body," the other replied.

"'Tis a *haole* body. Look at the red hair." The young boy picked up a stick and poked the body. "*Haole*, wake up."

"Tis a girl *haole*."

"Girl *haole* wears funny clothes."

The girl *haole* moaned.

"Run!" the first boy yelled as they both ran down the beach.

Spencer opened her eyes into small slits. Her eyes burned and the sunshine hammered a severe headache into her brain. "Oh, my God." She rolled to one side and emptied the contents of her stomach onto the sand beside her. "Where am I?"

Spencer propped herself on one elbow. She looked down the length of beach and saw two young boys several feet way. They stared at her with a look of trepidation on their faces. She reached her hand toward them. "Help!" she said.

"Run!" one of the boys yelled again and they ran farther down the beach.

"No! Come back. Please." Spencer felt a wave of dizziness overcome her before she succumbed once again to unconsciousness.

***

Spencer drifted in and out of consciousness and only caught random glimpses of her surroundings. She struggled to open her eyes briefly, and saw an elderly gentleman holding the occupants of the crowded room back with his staff. "Be gone with all of you. The *kähuna* needs room to work."

Kähuna. Where have I heard that word before? The Big Kähuna. Kevin Spacey and Danny DeVito. Spencer's thoughts wandered.

"The *haole* has lost a lot of blood. She will need several days of bed rest, and you'll need to get some fluids into her. The gash on her head was nearly to the bone. I've stitched it, but it will take some time to heal."

Spencer's eyes fluttered again. *Gash? Please come back. Don't run away! Help me!*

"Give her sips of this laudanum every few hours, and try to keep her quiet. I suspect when she is fully awake, she might become combative. Do you have any idea who she is?"

"Hanalei and Holokai found her on the beach. Some think she is a *wahine ho'okamakama*," the gentleman said.

"Why on earth would you think she's a prostitute?"

"Because of the way she was dressed when they found her. Doctor Wetmore, she was wearing next to nothing. A strip of cloth covered her top, and another covered the regions below, but she was naked otherwise. And she wore an odd red shirt with no sleeves. It was thick, like padding. We had to cut it off her."

Red shirt? What are they talking about? Spencer moved her head side to side and moaned.

"Chief, help me to lift her head. I'm going to give her a little more laudanum," Doctor Wetmore said. "She needs to stay quiet. She'll only do more damage to herself if she thrashes around." The doctor stood after administering the laudanum and looked at her patient. "She does look a bit odd. I've never seen a woman with her head shaved only on one side. I wonder if she belongs to a tribe."

"She is too pale to be anything but a *haole*. Look at how white her skin is—and her hair—it's red," the chief pointed out.

Doctor Wetmore nodded. "She's definitely not from here. My guess would be the mainland. Her coloring suggests she might be Irish, and most of them have been settling in Massachusetts after escaping the potato famine. The question is—what is she doing here and how did she land unconscious on your beach?"

"She is lucky Hanalei and Holokai found her. If the *'ōpiopio* found her instead, she would be dead right now—or worse."

"Those thieving, murdering pirates! King Kalakaua needs to do something about them before they destroy all of

Hawai'i. They have already brought deadly diseases to this land. Which reminds me, I didn't see any signs of leprosy on this one when I examined her."

The doctor and the chief stood for several moments in silence as they watched Spencer's laudanum-induced sleep.

"She seems peaceful now. Thank you for coming, Doctor Wetmore. I will send for you if things become worse."

"You're welcome, Chief. I will stop in to see her tomorrow."

Chapter 5

Spencer opened her eyes and looked around. She appeared to be in a hut, and she could hear sounds of the ocean nearby. She was alone. She lifted her head from the pillow and immediately lowered it again as an intense, stabbing pain shot through her head. She clutched her head with both hands. "Oh, my God." A sense of panic rose in her chest.

"Ah, you're awake!"

Spencer's attention was immediately drawn to the doorway where an attractive young woman stood. She had curly brown hair, a cleft chin and hazel eyes.

The woman crossed the room and stopped at her bedside. She extended her hand. "I'm Dr. Frances Wetmore. You can call me Frankie."

"Where am I?" Spencer asked.

Dr. Wetmore took Spencer's hand and shook it. "Nice to meet you. And you are…?"

Spencer frowned and locked gazes with the doctor. "I…I don't know."

"You don't know who you are? Do you know *where* you are?"

"No."

Dr. Wetmore hugged her sheaf of papers close to her chest. "I guess I shouldn't be surprised. You took quite a blow to the head."

Spencer tried to sit up, but once again, fell back when the intense pain shot through her head. She cried out.

"You need to settle down. You were found on the beach a few days ago. No one knows how you got there. Is there anything you can tell me about that?"

"I don't remember."

"What *do* you remember?" Dr. Wetmore asked.

Spencer looked around. Everything was new. Nothing was familiar. "I saw two young boys on the beach. They ran away. Doctor Wetmore, where am I?"

"Frankie. Call me Frankie. You are in the home of Chief Kanhanamoku in Princeville, on the island of Kauai, Hawai'i."

"What am I doing in Hawai'i?"

"I wish I could answer that question for you, but we don't know any more about you than you seem to know about yourself. All I know is that you were found on the beach a few days ago, injured, and wearing what appeared to be skimpy underclothing and a red, sleeveless, padded vest. I was hoping you could shed some light on this for us."

Spencer covered her face with her hands and wept.

Dr. Wetmore squeezed Spencer's shoulder. "Sweet girl, no need to cry. It isn't the end of the world. We just need to figure out who you are and how you got here. For now, you are safe."

"Will my memory come back?"

Dr. Wetmore sat on the edge of Spencer's bed, facing her. She placed her hand on Spencer's arm. "You have a head injury. It's not uncommon for someone to be disoriented, or have memory loss after an injury like this. Judging by the fact that you are still able to talk and you appear to be aware of your surroundings, I don't think there is any permanent brain damage. In most cases, memories return. It will take time."

"How much time?"

"It could be days, or weeks. You need to be patient."

"What if there's someone out there looking for me?"

"I've thought of that. Chief Kanhanamoku has sent a messenger to post a notice on the village board. If someone on the island knows you, they will come forward."

"And if no one comes?"

"Then we wait, and you heal, and eventually, your memories should return. I'm sorry if that causes your loved ones distress, but it is unavoidable if no one comes forward quickly. For now, you need to keep your wits about you and focus on healing."

Dr. Wetmore stood and cocked her head to the side. "You have a unique hair style. I'm willing to bet the redhead who emerges from your memory is going to be an interesting person."

Spencer reached up to feel the short crop of hair on one side of her head. "I have red hair?" she asked.

"Yes, you do. In fact, I've decided that will be your name—until we know better, of course." Dr. Wetmore took her hand once more. "Relax and let the natives spoil you while you heal, Red. You will find them to be a loving and caring people. I have to go now, but I will be back tomorrow."

Dr. Wetmore turned to leave and encountered Chief Kanhanamoku entering the hut. "Ah, Chief. Our patient is awake. Unfortunately, with no memory of who she is, or what happened to her, but that will return with time. I'm sure she's quite hungry, considering she's been out for a few days." Dr. Wetmore looked once more at Spencer. "I'll see you tomorrow, Red."

Chief Kanhanamoku watched the doctor leave and then turned his attention to Spencer. "Red? That is an unusual name, but fitting. I am Chief Kanhanamoku, leader of Princeville village. Welcome to my home, young lady."

***

Spencer sat up in bed with a tray straddling her legs. "Wow, that was amazing. What did you call it?" Spencer asked.

"Saimin. It is a noodle soup in a fish broth. It is one of my favorites when I'm not feeling well," Chief Kanhanamoku said. "It is a popular dish in the Kingdom of Hawai'i."

"Wait! What did you just say?"

The chief frowned. "I said it is a popular dish."

"Not that. You called Hawai'i a kingdom."

"Yes. That is what it is."

"But Hawai'i is a state. It was annexed by the United States in eighteen ninety-eight and then became a territory in nineteen hundred and a state in nineteen fifty-nine. I know this because I researched it before coming here."

Chief Kanhanamoku stood and walked across the room. He turned to face Spencer. "There has been talk of annexation, but it has not happened."

"It was annexed one hundred and twenty years ago. It became a state sixty years ago. How can you not know that?" Spencer was confused and more than a little agitated.

The chief approached her bed and took the tray away. "Maybe you should sleep. I'm sure you'll see things more clearly in the morning."

***

A cacophony of chirping birds woke Spencer in the morning. She brought one hand to her face to wipe the sleep from her eyes, and moaned involuntarily as the movement caused her arm and shoulder to ache. "Damn! I feel like I've been hit by a truck," she said beneath her breath.

Spencer threw back the covers and shifted her legs to the side of the bed. With a lot of effort and breath-taking pain, she managed to push herself into a seated position. Her head throbbed like a toothache as she sat on the side of the bed and fought the nausea that overcame her. She wrapped her arms around her mid-section and rested her torso on her thighs to regain her composure. It was in this position that Chief Kanhanamoku found her.

"*Aloha*! I see that you are awake, Red."

Spencer sat up and held herself steady by placing both hands on the bed beside her thighs. She turned pathetic eyes toward the chief.

The chief turned to the young lady who had followed him into the room with a platter of food for Spencer. "Go summon Dr. Wetmore."

Chief Kanhanamoku watched the maid place the platter on the bedside table and then scurry out of the room to do his bidding. He turned to Spencer. "I'm afraid you don't look very well. Maybe you should lie down again."

"No. I need to get up. I need to find out what happened to me."

The chief put a hand on her shoulder. "There will be time for that after you have healed. For now, you need to rest. Kalani has brought a delicious platter of food for your breakfast. Let me help you to sit back so you can enjoy it."

Spencer rubbed her face with both hands and then rested her forearms on her thighs. "Listen to me. I don't know who I am. I don't know *where* I am. I don't know what happened to me. I can't just lie here and not do anything about that."

"Yes you can, and yes you will," Dr. Wetmore said from the doorway. "Look, Red, you've had an accident and a pretty serious head injury. If you rush things too soon, you could end up with a disabling apoplexy. If that's what you want, then keep right on." The doctor stepped aside and pointed to the doorway.

Spencer lowered her chin to her chest and closed her eyes. Her shoulders shook as she wept silently.

Chief Kanhanamoku looked helplessly at Dr. Wetmore. Dr. Wetmore approached Spencer and sat on the bed beside her. She wrapped her arms around Spencer's shoulders and pulled her into an embrace. Spencer went willingly and allowed the tears to fall freely.

"It'll be okay, Red. I know it's scary right now, but it will get better. I know it will," Dr. Wetmore said.

"I'm scared."

"I know. I would be too if I were in your position. It's okay. There are lots of people here to help you through this."

Spencer pulled out of the doctor's embrace and sat upright. "I hurt everywhere. I wish I knew what happened to me."

"The only injury I found was the head wound, but considering the muscle pain you're experiencing I'm sure whatever caused it was quite catastrophic."

"I need to know what happened. I can't just lie here and do nothing."

Dr. Wetmore took Spencer's hand. "Look, I know you're anxious about this. I can't say that I blame you, but you will do yourself more harm if you don't give your body time to recover."

"I lay here last night for hours and tried to remember what happened. I drew a total blank except for one thing."

"And that is?" Dr. Wetmore asked.

"I remember being in the water and looking at someone who was leaning over the edge of a boat. I'm pretty sure it was a woman, judging by the way she was dressed. I remember seeing the most interesting tattoo on her chest."

"Tattoo?"

"Yes. It was a crescent moon with a trail of stars extending from it. The stars disappeared into her clothing, so I can only imagine where the trail ended." Spencer blushed.

Dr. Wetmore spared a nervous glance at Chief Kanhanamoku. "Maybe that memory will help to trigger more...after you heal, that is."

"How the hell will the memory of a tattoo help?" Spencer asked impatiently. "I don't even know my own name."

"I'll make a deal with you. Give it a week of rest, good food and following my advice, and then I will personally help you."

Spencer looked sideways at Dr. Wetmore. "You would do that for me?"

"Absolutely."

Spencer smiled. "Okay then, it's a deal."

Dr. Wetmore stood and faced Spencer. "Great! Now, back into bed with you."

Chapter 6

"Chief Kanhanamoku. Please, come in." Dr. Wetmore rose from her chair behind her desk and met the chief in the center of her office. "To what do I owe this pleasure?"

"May I?" The chief nodded in the direction of the couch on the opposite side of the room.

"Of course. Where are my manners? Please, have a seat."

The chief sat on the couch, while Dr. Wetmore sat facing him in a nearby chair. "What can I do for you, Chief?"

The chief shifted in his chair. "I came to discuss Red. I am concerned about her mental state."

"Her mental state? She's been through some sort of catastrophic accident. It is understandable that she is somewhat confused."

"Dr. Wetmore, she seems to believe that Hawai'i' is a member of the union. In fact, she claims it was given statehood sixty years ago."

Dr. Wetmore frowned. "Sixty years ago? Did she actually say that?"

"She did. She insisted on it. In fact, she said something about researching it before she came here. I have no idea what she meant by that."

"I'll speak with her about it, if you'd like," the doctor offered.

"That might be wise. She seems to be healing quite well and may be ready to move on in the next day or two."

"But she still has no memory of who she is or how she came to be here."

"True, but she seems determined to find out—with your help of course."

"I did promise I would help. I guess I need to start with another examination."

"What do you think about her memory recall?"

"Do you mean the tattoo?"

"Yes. I remember being suspicious from the day she was found on the beach that the bearer of that tattoo may have something to do with this young woman's injuries."

"I don't want to jump to conclusions, Chief, but I have to admit I was a bit startled when she mentioned the crescent moon," Dr. Wetmore said. "I don't want to trigger any immediate traumatic memories by asking her about it directly; those are better off coming out gradually, but I will feel the waters so to speak, and with any luck, we can confirm your suspicions. It might be a good jumping off point toward total memory recall for her."

"The question is—what can we do about it? I supposed I should give that some thought. I will discuss it with the council at our next meeting," the chief said.

"Until then, we need to do what we can to get Red back onto her feet. Thank you for coming in to voice your concerns, Chief."

The chief stood, but paused before leaving. "Part of me will be sorry to see her go. She has grown on me during the past week."

Dr. Wetmore smiled broadly. "I know what you mean. I feel a closeness to her that I generally do not allow with patients."

Chief Kanhanamoku put his hand on Dr. Wetmore's shoulder. "Could it be that she is a *makemake i nā wāhine*? I mean…the shaved hair, and the fact that she insists on wearing trousers."

Dr. Wetmore blushed. "My intuition tells me that she may be a *'o nā wāhine*. That would certainly explain the kinship I feel with her, but I hesitate to speak to her about it."

"Could I ask why?"

Dr. Wetmore rose from her chair and walked toward her desk. She picked up a black and white picture of herself and an attractive native woman in a loving embrace. A feeling of happiness passed through her chest. "She has no memory of who she is. I hesitate to plant suggestions like that into her brain, when it may turn out not to be true."

"I can certainly understand that. Nevertheless, her health has improved, and it is near time that she takes the next step—whatever that may be. Good day, Dr. Wetmore."

"Good day to you, Chief Kanhanamoku."

Dr. Wetmore placed the picture back on her desk and sat in her chair. She spent the next several moments with her eyes closed as she thought about the chief's red-headed visitor.

***

"How am I doing, Doc?"

Dr. Wetmore put her examination tools back into her bag. "I'd say you are one-hundred percent, although I am still concerned about your lack of memory." Dr. Wetmore sat on the edge of the bed. "Tell me again, Red—what do you remember before and after waking up in the chief's home."

Spencer sighed. "We've been through this several times already. I don't remember anything, other than the crescent moon tattoo. The next thing I knew, I woke up on the beach surrounded by two young boys, who ran away. My next memory was waking up in this bed. I don't know what else you want me to say."

Dr. Wetmore put her hand on Spencer's arm. "Please don't be angry. I know we've been through this before, but I hope that by repeated discussions, some memory may be triggered. Look, Red, Chief Kanhanamoku said something about your insistence that Hawai'i' is part of the United States."

"That's because it is," Spencer insisted.

"And when exactly did that happen?"

"Nineteen fifty-nine...nearly sixty years ago. You're an educated woman, Doc. You should know that."

"That's impossible," Dr. Wetmore said.

"Impossible? Why is that impossible?" Spencer demanded.

"Because this is the year of our Lord, eighteen eighty-four."

Spencer jumped out of bed. "No fucking way! No fucking way is this eighteen eighty-four. You're out of your fucking mind. Is this some kind of head game you're playing, Doc?"

"Calm down, Red. This is no game…and there is no need to curse. The year is eighteen eighty-four. What reason would I have to lie to you about that?"

Spencer ran her hand through her hair. "Do you have a computer I can use?"

"Computer?"

"Yes, a computer. You know…a laptop. Or a cell phone?"

The crease lines on Dr. Wetmore's forehead deepened. "Lap top? I have no idea what you're talking about."

Spencer became highly agitated. "I'm talking about a fucking laptop computer. Jesus! Do you all live in the stone-age around here?"

Dr. Wetmore crossed her arms. "No—not the stone age. We live in eighteen eighty-four."

Spencer turned sharply to face the doctor. "Stop saying that!"

"Okay, let's say that is it not eighteen eighty-four. What year is it then?" Dr. Wetmore challenged.

Spencer put her hands on her hips and cocked one eyebrow. "Two thousand nineteen."

"You think its two thousand nineteen?" Dr. Wetmore said incredulously.

"No…I *know* it's two thousand nineteen," Spencer insisted.

"Prove it."

Spencer marched to the door and flung it wide open. She stepped outside and stopped dead in her tracks. There in the harbor in the distance, were tall ships. On the street just a few feet in front of her were horse-drawn carriages. From one such carriage, a man wearing a linen suit, as well as a native woman wearing a colorful *holoku* dress, emerged from it. The road in front of the chief's home was packed dirt.

Spencer looked around at her wildly unfamiliar surroundings. "What the hell is going on?" she said out loud.

"Red. Come back inside."

Spencer turned around sharply to see Dr. Wetmore in the doorway. "I…I don't know what has happened to me," she said to the doctor.

Dr. Wetmore approached Spencer and took her hand. "Come. I promised to help you, and I will keep that promise, but first, we need to get your feet solidly on the ground. Maybe it's time you moved in with me."

***

Dr. Wetmore pushed the door to her cottage open and motioned to Spencer to go in before her. "Go on in. Make yourself at home."

Spencer walked timidly through the door and into the compact, but tidy kitchen. On one wall, there was a black gas stove with an oven, and on another, a sink with a manual water pump mounted beside it. A large window above the sink provided adequate lighting, and the deep sill provided a perch where a variety of herbs thrived in clay pots. A small kitchen table with four chairs was positioned in the center of the room. Above the stove and countertops, were open shelves on which stacks of dishes as well as non-perishable food supplies were stored. In a far corner, Spencer noted an icebox, where she assumed perishable foods were kept.

Dr. Wetmore noticed her looking at the icebox. "Nice, huh? It's state of the art. Oh, and right there, behind that wall, is the privy and bathing room. When I first bought this house, it had a backyard *hale li'ili'i* and no running water. Coming from the mainland, I was used to indoor plumbing, so I invested the time and money into updating this house. In our minds, it was worth every penny."

Spencer tilted her head in interest. "*Our* minds?"

"Huh?"

"You said '*our* minds'…as in more than one."

Dr. Wetmore's eyes flew open. "Oh! Yes. I guess since you'll be living here for the time being, you should know that there is one other person who lives here with me—my partner Leilani. She's out of town on island business right now."

Spencer stared at Dr. Wetmore for several long moments. Finally, she spoke. "Partner? As in business partner…or as in girlfriend, wife, better-half, bed-buddy, pillow-pal, card-carrying lesbian?"

"The latter…definitely the latter."

Spencer ran her hands through her hair. "Holy shit! I didn't see *that* coming!"

Dr. Wetmore's brow knit together. "Is that a problem?"

Spencer raised her arms out to the sides. "I…I honestly don't know! I have no idea how the real me feels about that. For now, I have no opinion."

"Hmm. Maybe I was wrong about you."

"Wrong about me, in what way? Oh, wait! Did you think *I* was a lesbian?"

"To be honest, I was leaning in that direction, but not sure. Are you?"

"Beats the shit out of me!"

Dr. Wetmore picked Spencer's bag up from the floor. "This is going to be interesting for sure. Come on, I'll show you to your room."

"Right behind you, Doc."

"Frankie. My name is Frankie."

Chapter 7

Frankie stood by the kitchen window and sipped a cup of coffee as she watched her guest do strange stretching exercises in the yard. She couldn't help but notice Spencer's taut midsection as she held one pose for several long moments. Frankie jumped when she felt a hand on her hip and then relaxed immediately when she felt a soft kiss on her cheek. She felt a warm body wrap itself around her from behind.

"Good morning, my love," Leilani whispered. She wrapped her arms around Frankie's middle and followed Frankie's gaze outside the window. "So this is Red, huh?"

"That's what I've been calling her. I have no idea what her real name is," Frankie replied.

"She has an interesting look about her. Do you think she is *ohaha*?"

"Do I think she's one of us? I'm pretty sure she is, but since she has no memory of who she is, I don't want to plant that idea in her head. She'll remember soon enough when her memories return."

"I'm sorry I wasn't here when you brought her home. The boat from O'ahu didn't dock until late. I'm afraid our guest was sleeping when I got home. In fact, you both were."

Leilani released Frankie and poured coffee from the metal filter pot.

Frankie turned and leaned her backside against the sink cabinet and allowed a warm feeling to invade her being as she looked at her partner. Leilani was slim, and taller than a typical native Hawai'ian. Her short cropped hair and androgynous style of dress did little to hide the fact that she preferred the fairer sex. Yet she held an important position on the Kauai Island Council, and it was in that capacity that she was sent to O'ahu earlier in the week. "I felt you slip into bed behind me when you came home last night. It felt good to have you home."

Leilani crossed the room again and placed a gentle kiss on Frankie's lips. "It is indeed good to be home. I missed you. By the way, thank you for sending word that Red was here. I might have worried that she was an intruder if I had come home and found her here not being aware of her presence."

"I'm glad the messenger found you before you left O'ahu. So did the Council of Island Kingdoms come to any decision about Makenna?"

"Unfortunately, no. They are hoping we won't need to use force to deal with her."

Frankie placed her palm on the side of Leilani's face. "Please don't tell me you volunteered for the job."

Leilani grinned and then ran a hand through her short hair. "No...not me. I was tempted, mind you, but she is too skilled for me. Confronting her will put me in an awkward situation. No—we need to find someone else to confront her. I don't think we'll get any more than one chance. The problem is that she hasn't done anything illegal...at least not yet."

"I find it incredible that there are still people like her in this day and age. Wasn't that all finished with about a hundred years ago?" Frankie asked.

"More like two hundred years ago. I think that's why she is so successful. No one knows how to deal with the likes of her anymore. She's been hovering on and off around the coast of O'ahu for about a week now. She comes and goes every few days...and she's making the chief of O'ahu nervous."

Frankie turned around and looked again at Spencer through the window. "I'm afraid our guest may have had an encounter with her."

Leilani frowned. "What do you mean?"

"Oh, it looks like she's finished with her exercise. She's on her way in."

Spencer stopped short when she entered the small kitchen. Frankie immediately approached her and inspected the bandage on Spencer's head.

"Come, sit." Frankie led her to the table and directed her into a chair. "How was the stretching?"

Spencer kept her gaze trained on Leilani through the entire exchange.

Frankie realized she had not introduced Spencer to her partner. "Oh, I'm sorry. Red, this is my partner, Leilani. Lei, this is Red." Frankie made the introduction as she attempted to remove Spencer's bandage.

Leilani crossed the room and accepted Spencer's firm handshake. How do you take your coffee?"

"Ow! Damn, Doc…that hurts!"

"Sorry, the scab is stuck to the gauze. I'll need to dampen it to get it off."

"Can't you just leave it on there?" Spencer asked.

"Nope. It needs to be changed. I'll be right back."

Spencer grinned at Leilani. "Is she always that stubborn?"

"You don't know the half of it!" Leilani replied. "Coffee?"

"Oh—yes. Black, please. Thanks."

Frankie returned with her medical bag. "Okay. Let's take another look at that wound."

Spencer sipped her coffee while Frankie worked to loosen her bandage. "This is good coffee, Leilani. Thank you."

"Thank Frankie. She made it while I was still in bed this morning. I'm afraid I got in pretty late. I apologize for not being here to meet you."

"No apology necessary. I am eternally in your and Doc's debt for allowing me to stay here. I'll be on my way as soon as Doc says it's okay."

"You're not going anywhere until your memory at least partially returns," Frankie said. "It's no problem for you to stay here."

"I second that, Red," Leilani said.

"Yow!" Spencer yelled.

"Finally!" Frankie held the detached bandage in her hand. "That was difficult to get off. Now sit still and let me clean the wound and put a new bandage on it."

"So, Red, how did you come to be on Kauai?" Leilani asked.

"I have no idea. I woke up on the beach with no memory of who I am or how I got there. I vaguely remember doing research about the island, but I don't know why."

"Research?" Leilani asked.

"Yeah. You know...I Googled the island...all of the islands in fact. Apparently, I am here as part of a planned visit of some sort."

Leilani raised her eyebrows. "Googoo? What is googoo?"

"Not googoo...Google. It's an internet search engine." Spencer looked back and forth between Leilani and Frankie and noted the looks of confusion on their faces. "Oh...right. I forgot. It's eighteen eighty-four." Frankie rolled her eyes sarcastically.

"Red thinks it's the year two thousand nineteen," Frankie said.

***

Spencer scooped a large forkful of scrambled eggs into her mouth. "This is good," she said.

"Thank you," Frankie replied.

"So, Red, what makes you think it's two thousand nineteen?" Leilani asked.

"Before the accident, it was two thousand nineteen. Don't ask me how I know that...I just do. I remember doing research about the islands before coming here, you know, to learn a little history so I wouldn't look like a total dorky tourist when I was here."

"So you are here intentionally," Leilani stated.

"Yes. I assume so. Anyway, Doc here told me it was eighteen eighty-four. I didn't believe her. To be honest, I still don't believe it. Part of me feels like I'm on a period movie set and any moment, the director will call a wrap and send us all home to our modern apartments and computers."

"I'm not sure what a movie is, or a computer for that matter, but I promise that what you see around you is real. And it *is* the year eighteen eighty-four. Frankie was not lying about that."

Spencer put her fork beside her plate and sat back. She stared at the hands in her lap for several long moments. "This is all so overwhelming. If I could only remember..."

"Give it time, Red. It will come back," Frankie assured her.

"You're obviously not an islander. Do you know where you're from?" Leilani asked.

Red shook her head without looking up.

"Based on her accent, my guess would be the northern states," Frankie said.

"That's quite a journey from there to Hawai'i," Leilani remarked. "Between the train ride across the country, followed by the boat ride to Hawai'i, it must have taken you a month."

"We flew. It took less than a day," Spencer replied.

"There is no way could you make to Hawai'i in less than a day. You're joking, right?" Leilani asked.

"Not at all. Like I said, we flew."

"What does that mean? You flew? Like a bird?"

Spencer nodded. "Yes. That's what I mean, only the airplane was much larger than a bird."

Leilani looked at Frankie. "Frankie, did you hear what she said? Could the head wound be causing such delusional thinking?"

Spencer leaned forward. "I'm not delusional, Leilani."

Frankie reached for Spencer's hand. "Lei didn't mean anything by that. She's just concerned about you...right, Lei?"

Leilani sat back in her chair and read the message Frankie silently communicated through her gaze. "Of course I didn't mean anything by it. I apologize." Leilani squeezed Spencer's upper arm. "And Frankie is right. I am concerned about you."

"Red, you said *we*," Frankie said.

Spencer was confused. "Huh?"

"You said *we* flew. Clearly that means someone else was with you while you traveled."

Spencer's forehead creased into a frown. "I did say that, didn't I?" She sat back and inhaled deeply. She looked back and forth between Frankie and Leilani. "That means I'm not here alone. I'm not alone."

Chapter 8

Spencer stepped into the kitchen holding an armful of clothing she had been given by the chief. She was wearing a very short *holoku* folded in half around her waist, and the string bikini top she was found in on the beach. Frankie and Leilani were at the sink, washing and drying the dishes they had used for breakfast.

"If you point me in the direction of the washing machine, I'll get my laundry done," Spencer said. "I'm running low on things to wear."

Leilani did a double take when she saw what Spencer was wearing. "Ah, I would not recommend going outside dressed like that."

"My goal is to wash these clothes so I don't have to. And by the way, what's wrong with what I'm wearing?" Spencer asked.

"Nothing if you don't mind being called a *wahine hookamakama*,"

"A hooka...what?" Spencer said.

Frankie handed the final plate to Leilani to dry before she addressed Spencer. "*Wahine hookamakama*. It means prostitute."

"Excuse me?" Spencer exclaimed.

"When the white man first began invading the islands, they offered money and goods to the Hawai'ian women in exchange for sex. The women dressed very much like you are right now to lure the sailors in," Frankie explained.

"But I've seen countless photographs of Hawai'ian women dressed like this," Spencer said in her own defense.

"You must have seen them on the mainland. We have seen few photographs here on the islands," Leilani said.

"Regardless, the folded *holoku* you are wearing is much too short, and the *maikai* barely covers your bosom and leaves little to the imagination. If your intention is to attract a mate, then subtle but flattering attire is more appropriate. The *holoku* needs to be won properly, no higher than knee level and more than just your nipples need to be covered by the garment you wear on top. Quite frankly, what you are wearing now..."

"This bra covers more than just my nipples!" Spencer exclaimed.

"Just barely. Look," Leilani continued, "I get that you're not from here, and heaven knows, where ever it is you are from, it might be common to dress like that, but here on the islands a certain reverence is due to the Goddess Pele, and reverence is expressed both internally, and by what we present externally."

"You guys don't wear knee-length *holokus*. In fact both of you wear men's attire."

"We are not your typical natives. Being *na wahine*, or lesbian has its advantages. The natives know where our hearts lie and because our preferences are similar to men, we can get away with dressing like men. Trousers are infinitely more comfortable than *holokus*."

"Your insistence on wearing trousers is what put thoughts in the chief's head about you possibly being *na wahine*," Frankie explained.

"He said that?" Spencer asked.

"Yes, he did."

Spencer tilted her head back and sighed. "Look...I'm not trying to attract a mate, and I have no clue if I'm *na wahine* or not. All I want to do is wash these clothes."

Frankie sought to rescue Spencer from her partner. She took Spencer's arm and led her to the back door that opened onto the lanai. "The wash and rinse basins and wringer are out here on the lanai. The soap is in the cabinet there. You can get water for the basins from the pump in the kitchen. If you'd rather use warm water, you'll need to heat it on the stove. The clothes can be hung over that line in the yard. The sun is strong here and they will dry in little time."

Spencer's brow creased into a deep furrow. "Are you telling me I have to wash these clothes by hand?"

"Is there another way?" Frankie asked.

"How about a washing machine?"

Frankie chuckled. "I'm afraid we are years away from getting such luxuries on the islands. We have recently heard news of electric clothes washers on the mainland, but here, we still do it the old fashioned way, with soap and a washboard."

"Ugh! You have to go through that process every time?"

"Every time," Leilani confirmed.

"I need to get more clothes. Is there any chance I can find work nearby? Work that will still afford me the time to figure out who I am and where I belong?"

"That's not a bad idea, but until then, I will lend you some of my clothes. We are about the same height, and heaven knows I have enough clothes to dress an army," Frankie said.

"I'll vouch for that," Leilani added.

"Okay. I appreciate that, but I still need to wash these." Spencer grimaced and pushed the door open to the lanai.

"*Aloha.*"

The greeting drew Leilani's and Frankie's attention to the main entry into the house.

"Papa!" Leilani said. She ran to her father and pressed her nose to his. Both of them inhaled at the same time to exchange the *ha*, breath, of life and to share their *mana*, or spiritual power between them.

"*Keikiwahine*, it is good to see you home. How was the meeting with the council?"

"Not good, Papa. They are nervous about the threat that lurks offshore. We will need to watch that situation closely and be ready to react if necessary."

"What do you propose we do? The last thing we need is a war, especially with Makenna."

"I don't have a solution, Papa. It is something the entire council will have to weigh in on. I only hope we have time to act before the opposition does. The council has agreed to convene in two weeks."

"Very good." He turned to address Frankie. "Dr. Wetmore, how is our patient?"

"Chief Kanhanamoku, don't you think it's time you call me Frankie?"

"No, I think Dr. Wetmore will do." The chief tweaked her nose and smiled. "It suits you. So, how is Red?"

"She's making a remarkable recovery. In fact, she talked this morning about finding work so that she has funds to buy clothing."

"Is that so?" the chief asked. "I may have some work for her. Let me give it some thought. For now, I need to get back to the congress and report on the council meeting."

"Maybe I should go with you, Papa. I can tell them firsthand what happened at the O'ahu meeting," Leilani said.

"That would be good, *keikiwahine.*"

Leilani kissed Frankie on the cheek. "I won't be long."

"I am making *loco moco* for dinner tonight," Frankie said.

Leilani grinned. "Then for sure, I won't be long. *Aloha.*"

"*Aloha,*" Frankie replied.

Spencer stood as still as possible on the lanai, just outside the kitchen door. She had listened with interest to the conversation going on just a few feet away.

So Leilani is the chief's daughter? I didn't see that coming!

I wonder what this threat is that sits offshore? Whatever it is, it sounds like it's bordering on war. I need to get out of here before something erupts that I can't escape. I need to find a way to get off this island and back to civilization. I don't know what's going on here, but this island appears to be beeping in a different orbit.

Chapter 9

Spencer came in from hanging her laundry on the line. "From this point on, I will forever to be in awe of the frontier women who had to wash clothes by hand," Spencer said. "Give me a Wi-Fi connected automatic washing machine and dryer any day."

Frankie shook her head. "You are an odd woman," she said.

Spencer raised her hands to the sides. "What?"

"You still think it's two thousand nineteen, huh?"

"I have to admit that it *looks* like the eighteen eighties here...at least what I think the eighteen eighties might look like, but I know things that you claim haven't happened yet."

Frankie thrust her palm forward. "Don't tell me. I don't want to know the future."

"So you believe me?" Spencer asked.

"I didn't say that, but even if it *is* possible, I don't think it's healthy to know the future."

Spencer looked around. "Where is Leilani?"

"She went to speak to the congress with the chief."

"You didn't tell me the chief was your father-in-law."

"Well, technically, Lei and I are not married."

"Yes. Of course not. According to you, it's eighteen eighty-four. Same sex marriage wasn't legalized in Hawaii until two thousand thirteen."

Frankie cocked her head to one side. "How is it that you can remember all these historical details that you say have happened, yet you don't remember your own name?"

"Beats the hell out of me. It's been what...two weeks since I was found on the beach, and I still don't know who I am. I'm here to tell you, that scares the shit out of me. I worry that I may never remember."

"Is it common for women to cuss all the time where you come from?" Frankie asked.

Spencer blushed. "I'm sorry. It's just that all of this scares me. I don't like feeling so vulnerable."

"You have also been cooped up either in the chief's house, or here for those two weeks. I think if you go out and about, something may trigger a memory."

"I'm glad you said that. I couldn't help but overhear Leilani say that she was going back to O'ahu in two weeks. I want to go with her."

"What do you expect to find on O'ahu?"

"Maybe nothing…maybe my memory."

"Red, you don't think you washed up on the shores of Kauai all the way from O'ahu, do you? O'ahu must be almost a hundred nautical miles from here."

"I…I don't know, Doc. To be honest, I'm looking for confirmation. I mean…I want to know if O'ahu is like *this*."

Frankie put her hands on her hips. "Are you suggesting that someone is intentionally making you think you're in eighteen eighty-four here, and you expect O'ahu to be in two thousand nineteen? You can't possibly think that is possible."

"I don't know what to think, Doc."

***

"Wow, Doc. This is good. What did you call it?"

"*Loco moco*. It's a popular Hawai'ian dish," Frankie replied.

"It's good, love," Leilani added. "You've outdone yourself this time."

"I tried a new recipe for the beef gravy. I'm glad you like it."

"I would have never put rice, a hamburger patty, a fried egg and beef gravy together in one dish, but damn…this is good. I'll have to remember this one when I get home," Spencer said.

Frankie reached across the table and took Leilani's hand. "I had to relearn how to cook when I met Lei."

"You're a fast learner," Leilani said.

"How did you two meet?" Spencer asked.

"I came to Kauai five years ago. I was on a retreat of sorts. I finished my schooling in America and then took a month off before starting a practice. As it turned out, the woman I was seeing at the time chose my graduation as an opportunity to leave me, so I came alone. That turned out to be fate because I had been in a relationship when I arrived here, I probably would not be with Lei today. Anyway, the chief talked me into staying on the island and to open a practice in Princeville."

Leilani squeezed her hand. "For me it was love at first sight. There before me was this petite, curly-haired angel. You stole my heart right from the start. Pele was certainly looking after my best interest when she brought you to Kauai."

"Praise, Pele," Frankie said.

A stabbing pain shot through Spencer's head. "Oh, my God!"

"Red, what is it?" Frankie asked.

"I…I don't know." *Praise Pele. Where have I heard that before?* Spencer closed her eyes and tried to make sense of the confusion that filled her mind. *Praise Pele. I see a celebration…maybe a wedding. What is happening here?*

"Red, are you okay?" Frankie asked again.

Spencer opened her eyes and looked at Frankie and then at Leilani. "I think I had a flashback. I was at a wedding. A Hawai'ian wedding. I can remember someone saying the phrase, 'Praise Pele'."

"Ah, and so it begins," Frankie said. "I think your memory is beginning to return."

"But it was just a flash," Spencer said.

"Or maybe it's a beginning," Leilani offered.

***

Spencer, Leilani and Frankie took a walk along the shore after dinner. At one point, Spencer lagged behind collecting seashells, as Leilani and Frankie continued along the shoreline.

"What do you make of Red's recall at dinner?" Leilani asked.

"It's obvious to me that her memories are beginning to come back," Frankie replied. "This could be a one-time event, or it might be a flood gate. Time will tell."

"Frankie, do you think it's possible…"

"Do I think it's possible that she's from the future?" Frankie finished her sentence for her.

"Well…do you?" Leilani asked.

"That's a pretty unrealistic concept."

"Yes, but still…"

"Hey, guys. Look at this awesome shell I found." Spencer ran to join them and then extended her palm to share her treasure.

"Wow, mother-of-pearl. That is a rare find," Leilani said.

Spencer shoved the shell into her pocket and then had to pull the waistband back up, as the action pushed them off her hips. "I need to get some clothes."

Frankie lifted the front of Spencer's shirt and tightened the drawstring around the waist band of the pants Spencer was wearing. "Sorry about that. We might be the same height, but you're thinner than me. There—that should do it," she added.

"Thanks. Don't get me wrong—I appreciate you lending them to me, but I need to find a job so I can buy some new clothes," Spencer said.

Leilani touched her arm. "I'm glad you brought that up. My father mentioned that he may have some work for you. Is there anything in particular you're interested in doing? Did you have any hobbies before you washed up on our shores?"

"Sorry. I'm drawing a blank on that one."

"That's okay. I'm sure Papa will find something for you to do. Do you feel like you're well enough to spend at least a few hours a day working?"

"Only a few hours? I was thinking maybe full time," Spencer said.

"Red, it's only been two weeks since you were found with a pretty severe head wound. I think part time is a good start. You can always add hours later when your body is ready to handle it," Frankie explained.

Leilani looked out across the ocean. "It looks like we're going to have a nice sunset. Maybe we should head back before it gets dark." She took Frankie's hand, and together, they walked side by side with Spencer, back in the direction they had come.

"So, Leilani, I understand that the chief wants you to go back to O'ahu in a couple of weeks," Spencer said.

"Yes, he does."

"I'd like to go with you. Maybe I can help with whatever it is you need to accomplish while you are there."

Leilani stopped walking. "I'm not sure that's a good idea. We are dealing with an issue that might be dangerous...especially for *haoles*."

"What's that supposed to mean?"

Leilani walked on, still hand-in-hand with Frankie. "Let's just say we are dealing with a hostile enemy...a native hostile enemy and I don't think it would be good for you to be there."

"Why not?"

"Well, for starters, it involves politics, and having a non-native involved may not be a good thing."

"I still want to go. I am hoping to find some answers to my memory loss there."

The three women walked in silence for the next few minutes. Finally, Leilani turned to Frankie. "What do you think?" she asked.

Frankie glanced at Spencer before answering. "Physically, she should be okay to travel in two weeks. I don't know that it will hurt her to go."

Leilani nodded. "I'll tell you what...why don't we all go? After my meetings, we can spend a few days on the island. It will like a mini-holiday."

"I'm good with that," Spencer said.

Chapter 10

"Papa told me I'd find you out here, Red. I see the chief is working your fingers to the bone," Leilani said.

Spencer looked up from the garden bed she was working in. "Hey, lady. Your father has been pretty easy to work for. I never would have thought I'd have a knack for gardening. I'm actually enjoying it."

"Did you remember to tell him that you would be going with me to O'ahu tomorrow?"

"Yes, I did. I can't believe how fast these two weeks have passed."

"Are you packed?"

"Yep! I knocked off a couple of hours early yesterday to do some clothes shopping. I appreciate Doc lending me some of her clothes, but it will feel good to wear duds that fit me."

"Speaking of Frankie, she wanted me to remind you not to be late for dinner. She's making *loco moco* again tonight. I think it's become her favorite new meal to make."

Spencer sat back on her heels. She cocked her head to one side. "You're a pretty lucky lady. You realize that, don't you?" she asked.

Leilani grinned. "I assume you're talking about Frankie?"

"Yes. I can see how much you love one another. It's in your gaze, your touch, your voice when you speak to her. I hope to find someone to connect to on that level someday."

Leilani squatted down in front of Spencer. "Maybe you already have, Red."

"What do you mean?"

"When your memories return, maybe there will be a Prince…or Princess waiting to reconnect with you."

Spencer absent mindedly drew circles in the soil in front of her with her spade. "I hope they have the patience to wait for me. It's been a month since the accident. I wouldn't blame them for moving on."

Leilani lifted Spencer's chin. "True love does not move on."

Spencer held her gaze for several moments. "I hope you're right."

Leilani stood. "Dinner's at five tonight. We need to get to bed relatively early. The ship leaves at six tomorrow morning."

"Don't worry. I'd walk on hot coals for Doc's *loco moco*. I'll be there on time."

***

"Oh, my God. Why did you let me eat so much?" Spencer sat back in one of the three lounge chairs positioned around a small fire they had lit on the beach, and rubbed her stomach.

"The way you dove into your dinner, I thought it was wise to keep my hands and feet away from the intake," Frankie joked.

"It was so good. Thank you for cooking, Doc."

"Are you ever going to call me Frankie?"

"Nope!"

"You can be so infuriating! And thank you, by the way. I love it when people enjoy my cooking."

Leilani reached for Frankie's hand. "Are you excited about tomorrow?" she asked.

"I am. It's been a while since I've been on O'ahu. I am looking forward to shopping."

Leilani chuckled. "Shopping? I should have known."

"I love shopping. How about you, Red?" Frankie asked.

Spencer frowned. "I don't know how I felt about it before I got here, but I enjoyed shopping for my new clothes this week."

"Good. You can come shopping with me while Lei is meeting with the council."

Leilani shook her head to warn Spencer off from the shopping trip, but stopped abruptly when Frankie nearly caught her.

Spencer missed the silent message. "Sounds like fun. I'm looking forward to it."

Leilani covered her eyes with one hand, lowered her chin to her chest and again shook her head.

Frankie glared at her. "What was that gesture for?"

Leilani tried hard to look innocent. "Nothing. Absolutely nothing. I'm sure you'll both have a great time shopping!"

Frankie patted Leilani's cheek. "I thought that's what you meant."

Silence fell on the trio as they watched the sun dip below the ocean horizon.

"Another beautiful sunset," Leilani said.

"Yes it was, but as much as I am enjoying the evening, we should think about turning in for the night. The alarm clock is set for five," Frankie pointed out.

***

Spencer tossed and turned well into the night. Finally, she settled on her back, closed her eyes and forced herself to relax. Soon, she felt herself begin to drift off.

Please come back to me, my love.

Spencer shifted in her sleep and unconsciously pulled the covers up to her neck.

I love you sweetheart.

Spencer frowned, but continued to sleep.

I miss seeing your beautiful green eyes. Please open them for me.

Spencer's eyes flew open.

Yes! I have missed you, ko'u aloha. *Welcome back.*

Spencer blinked her eyes a couple of times to focus her vision. There above her was a beautiful Hawai'ian woman with long dark hair and brown eyes. The woman was smiling broadly at her. There was something oddly familiar about her.

The woman lowered her face to Spencer's and kissed her tenderly. Spencer felt a jolting surge of desire fill her core with an intensity that took her by surprise.

All Spencer could do was blink. She had no voice. She was unable to move.

I see so much fear in your eyes, my love. Please don't worry. I will be here for you.

Spencer felt tears form in the corners of her eyes. Whoever this person was, she felt safe, and she felt loved.

Please don't cry. You are safe. Things will get better. I promise.

The woman kissed the tears from her eyes and then sat up. It was then that Spencer noticed something she had seen before. This woman had a crescent moon tattoo on her left breast, with a trail of stars that disappeared into her blouse. A phrase ran through Spencer's mind—*I am over the crescent moon in love with you.*

Spencer allowed an overwhelming feeling of love to fill her heart as tears poured from her eyes and into her ears. She found it difficult to breath, and she closed her eyes in an attempt to regain her composure. When she opened them again, the woman was gone.

"No. Come back," Spencer whispered into the dark. "Please, come back."

Chapter 11

Leilani placed a cup of coffee in front of Spencer. "Hey, are you all right? You're quiet this morning."

Spencer broke out of her trance and looked up at Leilani. "I'm sorry. I didn't sleep well. Things are a little foggy this morning. Thanks for the coffee, by the way."

"I'm sure you're just excited about the trip."

"You're probably right."

"Frankie is bathing, so you have about twenty minutes to finish your coffee before we leave. How about some toast for breakfast? I'm going to make a couple of slices for myself."

"If it's not too much trouble, I'd love some. Thank you."

"No problem."

Leilani stood at the stove and browned four pieces of bread in the open fire. She glanced over her shoulder at Spencer, who was once again, staring off into the distance. "Wanna tell me what's bothering you?" she asked.

Spencer snapped out of her trance. "Huh?"

"You seemed far away. Wanna talk about it?"

"Leilani, how much do the native people believe in dreams?"

"Wow, I didn't expect that question, but to answer, old Hawai'ian culture teaches that the human soul travels on journeys during the dream state. The Hawai'ian word for dream is *moe uhane,* and it means soul sleep. The elders believe that while dreaming, people communicate with their guardians. The guardians often take the form of sharks. Sharks are sacred in the Hawai'ian culture and are thought to be connected to family. If you dream of sharks...or if you are out at sea and you see sharks close by, it is a sign that a family member has sent it to you to counsel or protect."

"So things that happen during dreams are generally good?" Spencer asked.

"Not always. Some dreams have dark sides. The ancient Hawai'ians were afraid of becoming lost while dreaming. They also worried that their spirits could be controlled by shamans who could make them do terrible things. I guess you could assign the English word nightmare to those types of dreams."

Leilani watched Spencer closely. It was obvious to her that something was bothering her.

Leilani buttered the toast and placed them on two plates. She then retrieved the jam from the cupboard and carried their simple breakfast to the table. She sat down in the chair opposite Spencer.

"Here. Eat up while they're still warm."

"Thanks."

"Red, you'll feel better if you just talk about it."

Spencer sat back in her chair. "You're going to think I'm nuts."

Leilani chuckled. "Well, I've thought you were nuts from the beginning, so whatever you have to tell me will make no difference."

"That's right…the two thousand nineteen thing,"

"Exactly. So spill it."

Spencer leaned forward in her chair again. "I had a dream that left me a little shaken."

"Go on."

"For starters, I had a hard time falling asleep, and then when I finally drifted off, I heard someone talking to me and begging me to come back to them."

"Come back to them?"

"Yes. It was more like, 'come back to me, my love.' I assumed I was dreaming and tried to ignore it, but the voice persisted with declarations of love. Finally I opened my eyes. It took me a while to focus, but there, leaning above me, was the most beautiful woman I had ever seen."

"A woman?" Leilani prompted.

"Yes. She was amazingly beautiful. She had long dark hair and brown eyes…and she had Pacific Island features. I felt like I'd been run over by a truck. She took my breath away. I don't remember ever feeling that strongly about someone in my life."

"Well, I guess that answers the question about whether you are an *o nā wāhine*," Leilani observed.

"Do you think so?" Spencer asked.

"Look, Frankie has been working on that assumption from the first day you came to us, but she didn't want to put that idea into your head. She thought it was better for you to come to that conclusion yourself."

"Well, I gotta tell you, the woman in my dream took the wind out of my sails. The intensity of what I felt made me cry."

"So, did anything else happen?"

"I remember closing my eyes to fight off the tears and when I opened them, she was gone. I felt such an intense sense of loss. I begged her to come back, but she didn't. Oh, and there was one other thing. When she leaned above me, I noticed a crescent moon tattoo above her left breast. It had a trail of stars beneath it that disappeared into her blouse."

Leilani put both hands on the table and stood. She leaned toward Spencer. "Say that again?" she asked seriously.

"What part?"

"The tattoo. Describe it again."

"It was shaped like a crescent moon, and beneath it, was a trail of stars that looked like it might lead directly to her nipple."

"You're sure you saw it clearly?"

"As clearly as I am seeing you right now."

Leilani pushed away from the table and walked around the kitchen with her hands on her hips. Intense concern and worry were etched in her body language.

"Okay, you're freaking me out. What is so significant about that crescent moon tattoo?" Spencer demanded.

Frankie chose that moment to enter the kitchen, fully dressed for their trip. She stopped short when she saw Leilani and Spencer apparently in a stand-off. "What's going on here?" she asked.

Leilani pointed toward Spencer. "It appears Red here, has had an encounter with our problem child."

"Yes, I told you that," Frankie said.

"You told me that? Why don't I remember that conversation?"

"Because it wasn't a real conversation. Remember the day you got home, we were standing in the kitchen and Red was doing stretching exercises in the yard? That's when I told you. Red interrupted that conversation by coming into the house."

"Hello!" Spencer said. "I *am* right here, you know. You don't need to talk about me like I'm invisible."

"Wait a minute. Are you telling me she had this encounter *weeks* ago?" Leilani asked.

"Yes. When do you think the encounter happened?"

"Last night…in Red's dream."

Frankie looked at Spencer. "You had a dream about her? When you woke up from your accident a month ago, you told me you remembered seeing her leaning over the side of a boat looking at you in the water."

Spencer covered her face with her hands, rubbed hard to regain her composure and then lowered her hands to her hips. "Okay. Yes, I did see her leaning…and yes, I saw her in my dream. You obviously know who she is. Now spill it! Tell me who is she."

Leilani took a step toward Spencer. "Right now, the council believes she's our worst nightmare…and right now, I'm thinking you *know* who she is. Right now, I'm wondering why you appeared on our shore."

Spencer clenched her fists and held them close to her sides. Her face was a mask of anger and consternation.

Frankie stepped between them. "Lei, you can't be suggesting Red was intentionally planted here."

"How does it look to you, Frankie? She shows up here with a head injury and no memory of who she is or how she became injured. She wiggles her way into our lives…and into my father's home, and now we're heading to O'ahu, where coincidentally Makenna is hovering offshore. And now…the night before we leave for O'ahu, she sees a vision of her in her dreams. This smells like it's planned to me."

Rage and anger clouded Spencer's expression as Leilani accused her of being a spy.

Frankie came to Spencer's defense once more. "I can't imagine anyone intentionally inflicting a life-threatening injury like the one Red had when she was found on the beach. She could have died from that wound. That would have defeated the whole purpose of planting her here, don't you think?"

"What if her backers were counting on medical care being readily available? What if the beach she landed on was selected for just that reason? What if they are targeting the chief?"

"Lei, it could be a total coincidence that she washed up on shore in Princeville."

"Or maybe that beach was specifically chosen because they knew *you* in particular would be involved in her care?"

Frankie frowned. "You are making no sense at all. What significance do *I* play in this?" Frankie asked.

"All I'm saying is that someone could have done their homework and realized you are in a relationship with the chief's daughter." Leilani pointed at Spencer. "What better way for *her* to get close to the chief?"

"Oh, for goodness' sake, Lei. Do you hear yourself? You are grasping here."

"What other explanation could there be, Frankie?"

"I don't have the answers, Lei…and Red isn't able to provide them right now, so I say we give her the benefit of the doubt. You can't automatically assume guilt. We are a democracy. That's not what we do in the Kingdom of Hawai'i."

"You want to give her the benefit of doubt? Fine! We will go to O'ahu—and she will come with us. Better to have her where I can watch her than to expose my father, and the government of Kauai to sabotage." Leilani leaned in close to Spencer. "I will be watching you like a hawk, Red. One suspicious move and I will have you detained. Is that clear?"

Spencer narrowed her eyes. "You are wrong about me, Leilani. You are dead wrong."

"You had better hope so."

"We should probably get to the dock. The ship leaves in less than an hour," Frankie said.

Leilani glared at Spencer once more and then left the room to retrieve their bags.

Frankie turned to Spencer. "I'm sorry she treated you like that, Red."

"Part of me understands her need to protect the chief, but she is wrong about me, Doc."

Frankie nodded. "Give her time. For now, we've got to go."

Spencer took a few steps toward the guest room to get her bag but then stopped and turned around. "Doc? There's one thing I need to know."

"What's that?"

"Who is Makenna?"

Chapter 12

Spencer stood at the railing of the sailing ship docked in Hanalei Bay and watched the crew carry out their orders before they set sail. Frankie waited beside her as Leilani stood a few yards away talking with one of the crew's officers. Spencer saw her gesturing wildly, and once or twice, she looked or pointed toward Spencer.

"She's warning the crew about me, isn't she?" Spencer said.

Frankie glanced over her shoulder. "She's worried, Red. Please don't be angry with her. The best way to win her to your side is to not behave like she thinks you might."

"I would never hurt the chief. You know that, don't you?"

"I hope you wouldn't."

"But you're not convinced of that, are you?"

Frankie turned to face Spencer and leaned one elbow on the ship's railing. "I'd like to think I'm a good judge of character, Red. My gut tells me that even though you present a tough-guy façade, in reality, you wouldn't hurt a flea. But Lei does have a point."

"And that point is?"

"We know nothing about you. We don't know where you come from. We don't know who your people are. We don't have any history about where you grew up or where you've lived. Hell, we don't even know your name."

"Well, that makes three of us, Doc. If I knew, I would tell you."

Frankie nodded. "I suspect you would."

"What about Leilani?" Spencer asked.

"I recommend you keep to yourself on this trip to O'ahu. Keep it low-key. You're right—she has informed the crew of her suspicions, so don't give them anything to pin on you."

"How long will this trip be?"

"If we leave on time, we should arrive in Honolulu before dark. All in all, the trip should take eleven or twelve hours if the weather cooperates."

"And if the weather does not cooperate?"

"It could be as long as twenty or more hours."

"Twenty hours?"

"Yes. We need to sail all around Kauai from its northern most point here in Hanalei Bay to Kapa'a, then cut across about a hundred miles of open ocean, and then around the southwestern shores of O'ahu before we reach Honolulu in Mamala Bay on the southern shore. It's quite a long sail, and the ocean can be treacherous when the waves are high. If we're lucky, it will be smooth seas, and we'll get there in a reasonable amount of time."

***

Frankie walked to the doorway of the cabin and looked at Spencer, who had remained on deck since leaving Kauai.

"Is she still out there?" Leilani asked from where she sat at the table behind her.

"Yes, she is. I'm surprised she doesn't find shelter. The wind is pretty strong out there," Frankie replied.

"Her choice."

Frankie turned to look at Leilani. "Is it? You've done nothing to make her feel welcome."

"I don't know if I can trust her, Frankie."

"So in your eyes, she's guilty until proven innocent. Tell me—what has she done wrong?"

"It's not what she *has* done…it's what she *could* do."

Frankie swung around and approached Leilani. She planted her hands firmly on the table and leaned forward. "Listen to yourself. It's what she *could* do? Seriously? Since when do you judge someone by what is possible rather than what is real? When I first came to Kauai, there were a lot of things I *could* have done. As his doctor, I had free access to the chief. I could have done all sorts of harmful things to him...but I didn't. Did you silently mistrust me as much as you mistrust Red right now?"

Leilani studied her hands on the table before her as she listened to Frankie speak. When the lecture was over, she looked up and met Frankie's gaze. For a few moments, nothing was said. Finally, Leilani nodded. "You're right. You're right—I've been unfair. I...I just worry about Papa, and I worry about you."

Frankie cupped the side of Leilani's face. "Sweetheart, I love the way you protect us. I love that more than you know, but I'm a big girl who can take care of herself, and your father has plenty of protection around him whenever he is out in public. Lei, you have such a beautiful heart. I hate to see it so full of angst and suspicion, especially when it's directed at someone who may not deserve it."

"Red?"

"Yes. Do you know that before we set sail, she asked me who Makenna is? She has no idea."

Leilani stood and walked to the doorway. Frankie joined her and slipped her arm around Leilani's waist.

"It must be cold out there. I should probably invite her inside," Leilani said.

Frankie nodded. "I think that would be appropriate. I'll prepare a light lunch for the three of us and maybe we can knock this emotional wall down that has risen between us."

Leilani made her way quickly to the closest railing. The wind blowing as hard as it was made the ship heave up and down through the whitecaps. With a firm grasp on the railing, she slowly made her way to where Spencer stood. When she reached Spencer, she stood beside her and shoulder-bumped her.

Spencer jumped. "Jesus, you scared me!"

Leilani grinned. "Sorry about that. I'm on a mission. Frankie sent me out to get you. She's making lunch."

Spencer looked her directly in the eyes. "Frankie sent you out?"

"Okay, I confess. I volunteered. Look, Red, I don't have an excuse for the way I've been behaving around you all day, but I do have an explanation. I promise to tell you all about it, but right now, we need to get out of this weather and in where it's warm and dry. Boss-lady's orders. You don't want to get me fired, do you?"

Spencer entered the cabin and removed her cloak. She ran a hand through her stiff hair. "Damn. I'm covered from head to toe in salt," Spencer complained.

"It's from the whitecaps and mist in the air. There's a basin in the corner of the cabin if you want to wash before we eat." Franking pointed to a bowl and urn.

"So you two have a cabin of your own?" Spencer asked.

"It helps that my father is the chief," Leilani replied.

"Sweet!"

Frankie frowned at the odd expression.

"Sweet? What is sweet?"

"The cabin. You know…way cool! Awesome!"

"Does everyone talk as oddly as you where you come from," Leilani asked.

Spencer dried her face and arms. "Yeah. I guess we do."

"Come sit down. We have bread, meat and salad for lunch." Frankie retrieved three wooden plates from the cabinet and filled each one.

Leilani poured three mugs of wine and placed them in the center of the table.

Spencer sat and looked at their feast. "This looks good. Did you bring all of this from home?"

"Yes. Please enjoy it," Frankie replied.

For the first few minutes, silence prevailed as they ate their lunch. Halfway through, Leilani took a deep drink from her mug and put it on the table beside her plate. "Okay," she said. "I owe you an explanation."

"I'm listening," Spencer said.

"It's hard to know where to start," Leilani said. "Maybe a little history will help. More than one hundred and fifty years ago, when the first American traders came to the island, they exploited the people and the land. By the eighteen thirties the sugar trade took root.

"Next, came the American missionaries. They had a profound impact on Hawai'ian culture, and especially on Hawai'ian religion. By eighteen forty, the U.S. Government convinced the rulers to replace the traditional monarchy with a constitutional one, which basically reduced the Hawai'ian monarchs to powerless figureheads.

"What happened next confirmed for many natives that the United States was planning to overthrow the monarchy of Hawaii. In eighteen seventy-three, a little more than ten years ago, the U.S. military suggested they trade Ford Island for a tax-free import agreement of sugar from Hawai'i into the U.S. They argued that Hawai'i was strategically placed for the defense of the west coast of the United States. The U.S. military was willing to do anything to gain control of Pu'uloa, Pearl Harbor. Fortunately for native Hawai'ians, the monarch at the time, whose name was William Lunalilo, objected to selling the island and he officially opposed annexation of Ford Island.

"Then, just three months later—just when we thought Hawaii was safe—Lunalilo drank himself to death. He left no heirs, so the newly established constitutional monarchy elected David Kalakaua as monarch. He still rules today.

"The United States took advantage of the new ruler and pressured him to surrender Pearl Harbor to the U.S. Navy. The U.S. Government was relentless with their pressure on Kalakuau. He traveled to Washington, DC several times to work out a treaty, and finally, between Kalakuau and the U.S. Congress, they agreed to the Reciprocity Treaty of eighteen seventy-five, in exchange for Ford Island, of course."

Leilani sat back and sipped her wine.

"So, the new monarch agreed to hand them Pearl Harbor for a treaty concerning sugar imports?" Spencer asked.

"Basically, yes," Leilani replied. "Don't misunderstand me...the tax-free treaty *did* result in a sugarcane boom in Hawai'i and a large investment in Hawai'ian sugar plantations, especially by Americans, but many Hawai'ians were concerned it would lead to the annexation of Hawai'i.

"This was supposed to be a seven year treaty. It was set to expire two years ago, but has been re-negotiated on a year-by-year basis for the past two years."

"It seems to me that both the U.S. Government and the Hawai'ian people benefited from the treaty. Isn't that a good thing?" Spencer asked.

"You would *think* a boom in the sugar industry, which brought economic success to Hawai'i would be a good thing, but here's the problem: The United States' President Chester Arthur is in favor of modifying the treaty, and earlier this year, a proposal was sent to the Unites States Senate to extend the treaty for another seven years in exchange for exclusive use of Pearl Harbor by the U.S. Navy.

"The Council of Island Kingdoms is concerned that ratification of this new treaty extension will guarantee the annexation of the Kingdom of Hawai'i to the United States against the will of the Hawai'ian people. They fear that the United States—or forces backed by the United States—will actively remove the island monarchs from power, and take control of the islands.

"So now it is, eighteen eighty-four, and we are in the midst of fear and unrest among the Hawai'ian people. On one hand, they are fearful that we will lose our homeland, our traditions and our way of life if this treaty is extended, but on the other hand, the treaty has brought economic prosperity to the islands and would continue to do so for yet another seven years."

"It sounds like you're conflicted about this, Leilani," Spencer said.

"I won't deny that is true. There are other benefits to this treaty beside the sugar trade. It would also afford us protection by the United States against hostile invaders. It's not a black and white issue, unfortunately."

Spencer sat back and crossed her arms. "So what has this got to do with me? Why would any of this make you think I want to hurt the chief?"

"There are rumors of insurgents who are working against the monarchy. Many natives believe they are being funded by rich Americans. One of the insurgents is named Makenna. She is a ruthless pirate, and she has been hovering on and off in the waters beyond O'ahu for several weeks. The fact that she has apparently appeared to you in your dreams is concerning to me."

"How do you know she's one of the insurgents?" Spencer asked.

"She has a reputation for being ruthless. She's all about winning and taking the prize. Would she commit treasonous crimes if it paid well enough? I think she would. Why else would she be staging such an intimidating presence off-shore?"

"Why don't you just arrest her?"

"Because she hasn't committed any crimes in Hawai'i. At least not yet. She's just waiting out there in the harbor. We can't arrest her for being a bully unless she does something harmful or illegal. What she *is* doing, is making a lot of people nervous."

"I want to meet her," Spencer interjected.

Leilani stared at her in disbelief. "That is out of the question. Why on earth would you want to do that?"

"If it *was* her who appeared to me in my dreams, she may be the key to finding out who I am."

Frankie, who'd been passively listening to their conversation, piped in. "Maybe that's not a bad idea," she said.

Leilani turned quickly at the unexpected interruption by Frankie. "What did you say?"

"I said, maybe that's not a bad idea. What better way to get close to Makenna without her being suspicious that the authorities are on to her?"

"Whoa," Spencer said. "I'm not sure I want to get in the middle of your political unrest here. I just want to know what connection she has to my dreams."

Frankie leaned across the table. "Look, Red. If you want a chance to prove yourself, this might be it."

"It's too risky, Frankie," Leilani said. "We could be putting Red's life in danger here. We have no idea how Makenna would react to her."

Spencer held her hand up. "No...no, Doc may have a point there. I mean...I'm American. If the insurgency really is being funded by the U.S., that might give me an edge with her. I could approach her like I know she's one of the insurgents and convince her we're on the same team."

Leilani stood up and paced the cabin. "I don't know about this." She stopped and looked at Spencer. "What if she doesn't take kindly to you showing up and invading her space? Can you even defend yourself?"

Spencer reacted like she had been slapped. "Why should I have to defend myself?"

"Because she's a pirate?" Leilani said sarcastically.

"I...I don't know. I have no memory of having to defend myself. Maybe I should be armed just in case, although I'm not sure I could shoot someone."

Leilani paced again. She ran her hands through her hair. "Ugh! The more we talk about this, the more I hate the idea."

"The idea is to *appear* as if you can take care of yourself," Frankie suggested.

"What did you have in mind?" Spencer asked.

Frankie stood and walked to the center of the cabin. "Come here, Red."

Spencer pushed away from the table and joined Frankie in the center of the room while Leilani stood nearby.

Frankie walked in a circle around her and then stopped in front of her. "Okay. We dress you in leather trousers, knee-high boots, white buttoned shirt and a black vest. You can wear my Bulldog Derringer on your hip."

"You have a derringer?" Spencer asked incredulously.

"Yes. My father insisted on it when I came to Hawai'i. I always take it with me when we travel…just in case we have to defend ourselves, so as luck has it, I have it with me on this trip. We'll put it in a holster on one hip, and a sword on the other hip."

"Wait…a sword?" Spencer asked.

"Yes, of course. *She'll* be wearing a sword, so you should too."

Spencer put her hands on her hips. "Lovely. You're going to dress me like Errol Flynn."

"Dress you like who?" Leilani asked.

"Errol Flynn. He was an actor in the nineteen forties. He made a pretty convincing pirate."

Spencer was met with blank looks from both ladies. She shook her head. "Never mind. Do I get to wear a wide brimmed hat with a feather in it too?" she joked.

Frankie's eyes opened wide. "That's not a bad idea!"

"Oh, Jesus," Spencer moaned.

Chapter 13

The sun trimmed the underside of the clouds with a magnificent array of red, yellow and orange hues as the boat made its final approach toward Honolulu. Spencer stood at the rail and watched as white water exploded against the cliffs of Iroquois Point, awash in red from the setting sun. As they drew closer to shore, she studied the acres of volcanic rock that made the land appears more like a remote planet, than Earth.

"This is amazing," she said to Frankie, who stood by her side.

"I know. The first time I saw it, it made me cry. It was overwhelming," Frankie replied.

Spencer fought to see into the growing darkness as they sailed along the coast of the island. "What are those fields?" She pointed to acres upon acres of plants in neat rows planted from the shore, to the top of a volcano.

"They're most likely sugar cane," Frankie explained.

Their attention was drawn to the cabin doorway as Leilani called out to them. "How about giving me a hand packing our provisions? We'll be landing in the next half hour or so."

"I sure hope the captain can find his way in the dark. I can hardly see my hand in front of my face right now," Spencer said.

Frankie pointed into the distance. "See that light there? That's Honolulu Harbor. The closer we get, the easier it will be to see. The captain's done this a thousand times. Relax."

"Okay. I'll try. In the meantime, let's go pack."

***

From their perch on the deck, Spencer and Frankie watched the steady stream of workers walking back and forth between the ship's cargo hold and the dock, each time, laden with a bag or two of produce on their shoulder.

Frankie glanced at Spencer. "You're pretty quiet."

Spencer replied without looking at Frankie. "Yeah, well, this isn't what I was hoping for."

Frankie placed her hand on Spencer's. "I'm sorry, Red. I tried to tell you that Kauai wasn't in time delay. As you can see, it's eighteen eighty-four in Honolulu as well."

"You were right, unfortunately."

Silence fell between the two women for the next several minutes.

"I'm amazed there is so much activity on the dock this late at night. It's got to be at least eleven," Spencer said.

"Commerce never sleeps." Leilani arrived in time to hear Spencer's question. "It's better to do this now than in the heat of the day. Are you ready?"

Spencer hefted the carpet bag she had borrowed from the chief when she moved in with Frankie, and followed her friends down the gangplank to the dock.

Leilani put her bag down next to Frankie. "Wait here while I hire a carriage."

"So, what are the plans for tomorrow?" Spencer asked.

"Well, Lei has to meet with the council in the morning, so you and I need to go shopping."

"Right...Errol Flynn. I almost forgot."

Frankie frowned and opened her mouth to reply just as Leilani returned. "I've got a carriage. Let's go."

***

The next day, Frankie pushed the door to their room open with her hip. She dropped her bags on the couch in the common room and then returned to the hallway to help Spencer carry the remaining purchases into the room.

"Thanks!" Spencer handed her two of the many bundles she was attempting to juggle. She followed Frankie into the room and pushed the door closed behind her. "I never would have thought when we left this morning that we'd buy so much."

"We're going to be here for a week, and maybe longer, depending on how the talks go with the island council. I thought it might be safe to get provisions for the week in one trip."

Spencer carried two bags of groceries to the kitchen area. "Let me help you put these away," she said.

Frankie took the bags from her. "No, I'll do that. I'd like to see you in your new outfits. Why don't you go try them on while I put the food away?"

"Do I have to? Really?" Spencer whined.

Frankie shook her head. "You are so much like Lei," she replied. "Yes...you have to. Now scoot!"

"Sheesh!" Spencer grabbed two of the bags from the couch, dragged herself across the room like a reluctant, petulant child, and disappeared into one of the bedrooms.

Just then, the door to the room swung open, admitting Leilani. "Hey, love," she called from across the room.

Frankie turned around and smiled. "Hey, baby. How was the council meeting?"

Leilani strode across the room and took Frankie into her arms. She held her close for several long moments and then kissed her gently. "I missed you today."

"I missed you too. So...again—how was the council meeting?"

Leilani released Frankie and leaned against the countertop as Frankie went back to putting groceries away. "It went as well as expected, I suppose. I'm not surprised that they haven't made any progress during the past two weeks on how to move forward with the Makenna issue. It's as though they were waiting for me to return—which I guess is a good thing."

"Maybe they were," Frankie observed.

"It's more likely they don't know how to deal with her. They are, after all, a group of older, traditionalist men. They aren't accustomed to dealing with aggressive women."

Frankie grinned and stood on tip toe to place a quick kiss on Leilani's lips. "My point. It takes an aggressive woman to deal with an aggressive woman, and they are smart enough to realize that."

Leilani frowned. "Do you think I'm aggressive?"

"Does the sun rise above Haleakala?" Frankie joked.

"Very funny."

"Did you tell them about Red and our plan to use her to get close to Makenna?"

"I told them."

"And?"

"And I'm not sure they like the idea any more than I do. It's risky."

"I'm not sure about it either," Frankie admitted. "But she might be our best shot. I do think we need to understand if she can defend herself before we feed her to the she-wolf."

"Speaking of Red, where is she?"

"She's in her room, trying on her new clothes."

"That's right. I forgot you two went clothes shopping today. How did you do?"

"I think we did great, but then you can decide for yourself when she comes out to model for us."

As if on cue, the door to Spencer's room opened and she walked into the common room.

Leilani's jaw dropped and she stood up straight when she saw her. Leilani's reaction caused Frankie to turn around.

Spencer was dressed in black, form-fitting leather pants, tucked into knee-high boots with buckles near her knees. She wore a black leather vest atop a white button-down shirt, with ruffles at the neck and ruffles at the wrists that extended beyond her coat sleeves. Her coat extended to mid-thigh and was decorated with a column of buttons on each side. The jacket had a stand-up collar and was clearly designed to be worn open.

"Wow! In the name of Pele, you look amazing!" Frankie said. "Don't you think, Lei?"

Leilani was speechless.

"Lei?"

Frankie's voice shook Leilani out of her stupor. "Ah...wow is an understatement. You are sexy in that outfit!"

Frankie lightly punched Leilani in the stomach. "Excuse me? I am right here in front of you, you know!"

Leilani rubbed her stomach while pointing to Spencer with the other hand. "Tell me she isn't sexy!"

"Yes, I admit she looks sexy. Now put your eyes back into their sockets, if you don't mind!"

"Sorry, Frankie. You asked my opinion."

Spencer's cheeks tinged with pink as she graciously accepted Leilani's praise. "I feel like we're getting ready for a Halloween party," she said.

Leilani approached Spencer and stood in front of her. She reached forward and released the first two buttons of Spencer's shirt and spread the collar wide. "That's better."

Spencer looked down at her exposed cleavage and then back up at Leilani. "You can't be serious."

"You need to get her attention. That should do it," Leilani pointed out. She turned to Frankie. "What do you think?"

"Give me a minute. I'll be right back." Frankie went into the bedroom she shared with Leilani and returned a moment later. She handed a holstered derringer to Spencer. "Here. Put this on."

"I don't know about this," Spencer said tentatively.

"If all goes well, you'll never have to use it," Frankie said.

Spencer raised her eyebrows. "If all goes well? That sure helps my confidence!"

Frankie pushed Spencer's coat back and hung the belted holster low on Spencer's waist. She tied the bottom of the holster to Spencer's leg by the rawhide straps attached to it.

Frankie stepped back to admire her handiwork. "Oh! One more thing...the sword. Lei, could you please grab it for me? It's on the couch."

Leilani picked the sword up and carried it to Frankie. "This is the real deal. Papa has one similar to it hanging above his fireplace. Where did you find it?"

"In the marketplace. Give me the scabbard, if you would," Frankie said to Leilani.

Frankie looked at Spencer. "You're right handed?"

Spencer nodded.

"Okay. We'll hang this on your left hip then."

Spencer held her coat back so Frankie could secure the scabbard unhindered. Finally, Frankie took the sword from Leilani and handed it to Spencer.

Spencer tentatively reached for the sword with her right hand. Her hand slipped effortlessly into the knuckle-bow between the cross guard and pommel, and her fingers and palm wrapped around the hilt with ease. Instinctively, she stood tall, with her heels touching, and held the sword straight out in front of her. The blade was a meter long and gently curved upward, ending in a sharp point. She stood there as though in a trance...unblinking.

A quick movement to her left caused her to set her mark, followed by a thrust while extending her front leg. Using a slight kicking motion, she propelled her body forward with her back leg and followed through with a straight thrust, counter-disengage attack and cutover.

"Red! Red, stop!"

Spencer was brought back to reality by the sound of Frankie's voice. She blinked wildly until Frankie's face came into focus.

"Red. Put the sword down. Put it down, now!"

Spencer looked around frantically and realized she was still in eighteen eighty-four...in a hotel room on O'ahu...and she had Leilani pinned to the wall at sword point.

***

Spencer paced back and forth in her room as she listened to the heated conversation going on in the room next door.

"It was like she was in a trance or something."

Spencer recognized Leilani's voice.

"I know. It happened when she took the sword. It's like something came over her. I don't think she realized what she was doing, Lei."

"Frankie, she could have killed me!"

"Yes, she could have, but she didn't."

"I don't know if I can trust her. I mean, what if she goes mad every time she handles that sword?"

"I don't think she's going mad, Lei. I think she is beginning to remember...at least her body is remembering. By the way she handled that sword, it's obvious she knows how to use it."

"All the more reason not to trust her, Frankie. I'm afraid when her memory *does* return, things are not going to work out as we'd like them to."

Spencer sat on the end of the bed and held her head in her hands. *What if Leilani is right about me? I wish I could remember.*

***

Spencer stood in the window of her room. A full moon cast an eerie glow across everything and despite the wee hours of the morning, the light appeared to hover between dusk and dawn.

She sighed deeply and then crept quietly through the common room to collect the things she had purchased that day. She returned to her room and stuffed her belongings in the carpet bag. Finally, she scribed a few words on a piece of parchment and placed it on her pillow.

Spencer quietly opened her window and thanked Pele that their room was on the ground floor. She leaned over the sill and placed her belongings on the ground under the window, and then climbed out after them. Soon, she disappeared into the shadows of the night.

Chapter 14

Spencer went directly to the docks after leaving the hotel. Even in the middle of the night, it was a bustle of activity. She made her way to the end of the dock and scanned the ocean horizon, where in the dim light of the full moon, she was able to make out the silhouette of a large ship, moored off the shore of Diamond Head.

"What's your business?"

Spencer swung around and came face to face with a tall, bristly-chinned longshoreman.

"Huh?" Spencer stammered.

"What's your business? This dock is private property."

Spencer had to think fast. "I, uh, I'm looking for work."

The man laughed heartily. "You're nothing but a little wisp of a girl. There's nothing here for you. Be gone with you."

Spencer grabbed his arm when he turned to walk away. "Wait. Give me a chance. I'm stronger than I look. I...I need the money."

The man looked her up and down. He noted the gun on her hip and the sword she had slung over her shoulder. "Are those yours?" he asked.

Spencer glanced at her weapons. "Yes, they are."

He crossed his arms in front of him. "I assume you know how to use them?"

"Yes sir, I do." Spencer replied and hoped the lie didn't show on her face.

The longshoreman studied her face. Spencer squirmed under his scrutiny.

"Well?" Spencer prompted.

"As it turns out, we are looking for someone to monitor security on the docks. Does that sound like something you'd be willing to do?"

Spencer swallowed hard.

"I need an answer, girl. If you're not willing, then be gone with you."

"No! No…I mean, yes! I am willing to do that."

The longshoreman extended his hand to Spencer. "All right then. My name is William, but the crew calls me Bear."

Spencer shook his hand firmly. "Red. My name is Red."

Bear chuckled. "It suits you. Now, come with me and I'll introduce you to the rest of the crew. Then you can show us what you can do."

***

Frankie set up the coffee pot to boil just as Leilani entered the common room from the bedroom. "Good morning, love. How did you sleep?"

Leilani crossed the room and kissed Frankie on the cheek. "Not too bad, considering the events of the past evening." Leilani pulled open the collar of her blouse. "Look at the bruise she gave me at the point of that sword."

Frankie looked at the angry mark above Leilani's left breast. "Damn. It almost broke the skin."

"Yes it did." She glanced at the door to Spencer's room. "Has she shown her face yet?"

"I haven't seen her," Frankie replied.

Leilani walked toward Spencer's room. "I'm a little concerned about leaving you here alone with her while I'm in meetings."

"Darling, I'll be fine. I don't think she meant to hurt you."

"Well, I don't like taking chances." Leilani pushed the door to Spencer's room open and looked inside. "She's not here."

"What?" Frankie quickly crossed the room and confirmed Leilani's observation. "I wonder where she went? Look, there's a note on her pillow."

Leilani looked around the room while Frankie retrieved the note. "All her stuff is gone as well, Frankie. Including the sword and your gun."

Frankie picked up the note from Spencer's pillow and then slowly sat on the edge of the bed as she read it.

Leilani sat beside her. "What does the note say?"

"It simply says, 'I'm sorry. Thank you for all you've done.'"

Leilani jumped to her feet. "I need to alert the authorities."

"And tell them what? That she has delusions about being from the year two thousand nineteen? What has she done that would justify arresting her?" Frankie asked.

"How about, she stole your gun? How about she's an armed lunatic?" Leilani suggested angrily. "And what about the sword?"

"The sword is hers. She bought it. And as far as the gun is concerned, I didn't tell her she *couldn't* take it. Hell, I was the one who made her put it on."

Leilani took Frankie by the shoulders. "Why are you defending her? She could be dangerous, Frankie. She could ruin everything for all of us!"

"You don't know that, Lei. I spent two full weeks with her before you came home. She is not a dangerous person. She has asked us to trust her. I think we should give her a chance."

Leilani walked a few feet away and then turned sharply back toward Frankie. "I don't understand what spell she has cast on you, Frankie. Is there something you need to tell me?"

***

Bear escorted Spencer to the main dock where about a dozen workers were assembled for an early morning breakfast. "Gather round," Bear shouted.

He pushed Spencer in front of the men. "This is Red. She is looking for a job."

Spencer's anxiety escalated when the men laughed at Bear's proclamation.

"That's enough," Bear said. "She deserves the same chance each one of you had. Now, you're all aware of the problems we've had with pirates lately, so I am considering putting her in charge of security on the dock. Red here says she's pretty good with a sword, so I thought I'd let her demonstrate her skills. Any volunteers?"

"I'll challenge her, Bear."

Spencer narrowed her eyes at her opponent...a young man who looked to be in his twenties. He was taller than her by several inches, and had sinewy muscles.

"Donovan. I suspected you would," Bear said. "Grab your sword."

Spencer took advantage of Donovan's brief absence to remove her coat, and the derringer on her hip. She shoved the gun and holster into her bag and asked Bear to keep an eye on her belongings while she engaged Donovan. She then unsheathed her sword from its scabbard and tossed the scabbard aside.

The dock workers cleared a large space and arranged benches in an oval shape to watch the engagement.

Spencer, standing at one end of the oval, slipped her hand into the knuckle-bow and gripped the hilt tightly. She closed her eyes and inhaled deeply. A searing pain shot through her temples and she dropped to her knees. As she fought the pain, she saw in her mind's eye, two people engaging in swordplay. She realized quickly that she was one of the participants, and that a mask hid the identity of her opponent. They parried back and forth several times until her opponent stuck her in the center of her chest. She immediately froze, knowing the match was finished...and knowing she was as good as dead. She looked up and watched her opponent remove the mask.

"Mak?" she whispered.

The cry from her more immediate opponent snapped Spencer into action. She rose to her feet and immediately deflected Donovan's thrusting sword with a circle parry. By deflecting his oncoming attempt, Spencer threw him off balance and he nearly fell, prompting a round of laughter from the onlookers.

"You bitch!" Donovan, wild with anger, lunged at her again.

Spencer executed a counterattack by moving back out of the way of Donovan's attack while scoring a strike on his arm. He came back at her time and time again; his sword swinging wildly in all directions as he screamed his fury. Spencer recognized that Donovan's repeated attacks were being driven by anger rather than skill, and she used this to her advantage by skillfully timing her deflections to minimize the impact of contact.

When it became obvious to Spencer that Donovan was beginning to tire, she executed a basic thrust with a cutting action, followed by several feints to throw him off guard. Again, Donovan nearly fell as he threw all his weight into an attack that missed his mark.

Spencer extended her front leg in a kicking motion and propelled her body forward with her back leg, while thrusting her sword and beating back Donovan's blade. Finally, she circled her blade around Donovan's blade and caught the knuckle-bow with the tip of her sword. In one swift motion, she tore Donovan's sword out of his hand and sent it flying across the dock, and at the same time she slipped her left foot between his legs, and tripped him up. In a few seconds, he was on his back on the ground, with the tip of Spencer's sword pinning him down.

"Stay down," Spencer warned. "Stay down. I don't want to hurt you."

Donovan's anger got the best of him and he lunged upward, effectively driving the point of Spencer's sword deep enough to draw blood. He screamed in pain and frustration.

Spencer withdrew her blade and bent over him. "I said to stay down, asshole! I could have killed you!"

Silence fell on the dock as Spencer extended her hand to Donovan. He looked at her hand, and then into her face, before he reached up and accepted her help. She pulled him into a standing position and they stood face to face.

Donovan held one hand to his chest to stem the flow of blood that was darkening his shirt. He placed the other hand on her shoulder. "Welcome to the crew, Red."

A cheer rose up from the crowd and they gathered around Spencer to congratulate her. Spencer looked through the crowd and caught Bear gazing at her. He winked at her and nodded.

"Okay, ladies. Back to work!" Bear bellowed. "Donovan, go and get that wound stitched. Red, follow me and I'll show you to your quarters."

***

Spencer closed the door behind Bear and threw herself on the bed. She was shaking like a leaf.

Where the hell did that come from? How is it I know how to handle a sword so well? Damn, I wish I could remember.

Spencer thought back to the encounter with Leilani in the hotel room the night before. *I could have hurt her. Maybe it's better that I left.*

She looked around the room. It was sparsely decorated, containing only a bed and a small table and chair. Beside the bed was a crude shelf unit, apparently for clothing or personal items. There was a small window on one wall that overlooked the harbor. She propped herself on one elbow and looked at the ocean, but she had a limited view from her perch on the bed. Hoping to see more up close, she sat up, and then made her way on shaky legs to the window. From where she stood, she could see the entire length of the coast, all the way to Diamond Head. The morning sun shone brightly overhead and it clearly illuminated the large ship moored off the coast that she had seen in the moonlight the night before.

Spencer sat in the only chair in the room and lowered her head into her hands. She tried hard to recall the vision she had seen just before her confrontation with Donovan. She was fencing—of that she was sure—but when, and where? And who was she fencing with?

Spencer rubbed her face and sat back in the chair. Her attention fell on the sword that she had dropped to the floor with the rest of her belongings just inside the door. She rose from her chair and retrieved the sword, which was sheathed in its scabbard. She carried it back to the table and sat down once more. With one hand on the hilt and the other on the scabbard, she withdrew the sword and held it before her.

A face flashed through her mind. It was the face of a beautiful native woman with long brown hair and dark eyes. An intense rush of emotion filled her chest, making it difficult to breathe.

"Mak…"

Chapter 15

Bear made plans to meet Spencer right after lunch to show her around the docks. He carried a large ring of keys that he used to access multiple warehouses along the route.

"How on earth do you remember which key goes to which lock?" Spencer asked.

Bear held up the key ring. "That's easy. As you can see, the warehouses are all in a row along the dock. The trick is that the keys are in the same order on the ring as the warehouses are on the dock. The warehouse number is on the door, so all you need to do is count the number of keys until you get to the one that matches the number on the door."

Spencer shook her head and laughed. "And here I thought you had magical powers."

"Don't tell the guys, all right? I don't want them to think the boss is human."

"Your secret is safe with me!"

They walked in silence to the next warehouse. When they reached the door, Bear turned to Spencer. "You gained a lot of credibility with the crew when you beat Donovan today...especially when you helped him up after defeating him."

"I wasn't trying to hurt him, Bear. It was supposed to be a friendly match. Believe me, if it was a life or death situation, the outcome would have been different."

"Have you ever killed a man, Red?"

"Not that I am aware of."

"Well, let's hope you'll never have to go there."

"Bear, you mentioned a problem with pirates. Can you give me a little more information about that?"

"It's not that we've *had* problems with pirates...it's more that we want to safeguard *against* having problems with pirates."

"Any pirate in particular that's giving you heartburn?" Spencer asked.

Bear put his hand on Spencer's shoulder. "Come with me."

Spencer followed Bear to the end of the dock. He stood beside her and pointed in the direction of Diamond Head.

"Do you see that ship out there?"

"Yes."

"We have reason to believe it belongs to the pirate Makenna."

"Makenna? What's his story?"

"*Her* story. Makenna is a woman."

Spencer pretended she was not already privy to that information. "A woman pirate? Really?"

"Yes."

"So, why hasn't she been arrested?"

"Because she hasn't done anything...yet."

"Well then, how do you know she's a pirate if she hasn't pillaged anything?"

"Her reputation precedes her."

"How long has she been moored there?"

"She's been coming and going. She was spotted off the shores of Kauai about a month ago, and then in early November, her ship was seen sailing by O'ahu, when it did an about face and slowly made its way into the harbor here. It came in so slowly, it looked as though she had mechanical problems, but so far, no one has ventured off the ship. She's been moored there for two weeks."

Spencer shaded her eyes from the sun with her hand as she looked at the ship. "It doesn't look like a pirate ship. Are you sure that's her?"

"You're right about that. It's a steam whaler. But, yes, we're pretty sure it's Makenna. She probably pillaged the ship from an unsuspecting whaler."

"So, I assume she's one of the bad guys you expect me to protect the docks against?"

"I suspect you wouldn't last long against her. She's no Donovan—that's for sure. She most likely has an armed crew as well, so no—I wouldn't expect you to personally defend the docks against her, but if you see anything suspicious happening around that ship, I would expect you to report it."

"Fair enough."

Bear and Spencer turned back to walk toward the warehouses.

"Bear, I've been hearing stories about unrest having to do with a deal the U.S. Government is trying to work with the kingdom. Something about Pearl Harbor?" Spencer prompted.

"You've been hearing right. The Navy wants to set up a strategic base on Pearl Harbor, but the natives don't want to give up the land. There is an attractive trade treaty being offered to the monarchy in exchange for the land, but so far, the king doesn't want to commit to anything permanent."

"But wouldn't a trade treaty be beneficial to the people of Hawai'i?" Spencer asked.

"Yes. It would. That's why there is unrest. You see, there has been a temporary treaty in place for the past several years and this latest offer is to make it permanent. The people are becoming wealthier and they don't want to see that stop. Some of them are forming insurgent groups to fight the monarchy."

"So how do *you* feel about this, Bear? I mean...I can't help but notice that you and the entire crew are *haoles*. None of you are natives."

"We work for an American company. All of us came here from the mainland. I would be lying if I said I didn't support the treaty. All of these warehouses are full of sugar cane that is destined for the United States. Trade between Hawai'i and the mainland is what keeps us employed...and now that includes you as well."

"I will do my best to protect these docks from thieves, marauders, and pirates. You have my word on that."

Spencer extended her hand for a firm shake.

"I appreciate that, Red. Here are the keys. Since most of the cargo activity on this particular dock occurs at night, there is always someone around to discourage thieves, so your hours will cover mid-morning until dark. Most of the men live in the crew quarters, so if something significant happens, we're only a shout away."

***

Spencer quickly fell into the routine of making her rounds three times a day to inspect each warehouse for evidence of forced entry or vagrant loitering. At Bear's request, she wore both her sword and Frankie's gun while doing her rounds. At the end of each round, she spent a full hour standing at the end of the dock, scanning the area around the moored ship for signs of movement, using a collapsible monocular she had borrowed from one of the dock workers.

After three days on the job, she had spent a total of nine hours watching for movement on the steam whaler, but had yet to witness any activity on the ship. As dusk approached on the third day, she closed the monocular and slipped it into her coat pocket. She turned to head back to her room, only to be stopped short by Frankie, who managed to walk right up to where she was standing, unaware.

"Jesus, you scared me!" Spencer exclaimed.

"Some security guard you are! You were so absorbed in what you were looking at that I walked right up to you undetected," Frankie said.

"How did you find me?"

"I've known where you were for the past three days. It's not often a red-haired *haole* woman sporting a sword and a gun shows up out of the blue. It wasn't hard to track you down."

Spencer studied the boards on the deck; too ashamed to look directly at Frankie. "I'm sorry I cut out on you. I didn't know what else to do. I'm pretty sure after the sword incident that Leilani would have had me arrested if I stuck around."

"Red, look at me."

Spencer reluctantly obeyed.

"Lei would not have had you arrested. For starters, I wouldn't have let her. You didn't do anything wrong."

"I had her pinned to the wall with my sword. Where I come from, that's called assault."

"Yes, but there were extenuating circumstances. In my humble medical opinion, what happened was caused by muscle memory. You are obviously well skilled with a sword, and even if your brain doesn't acknowledge it, it appears your body does."

"She must be angry with me."

"She's angrier with *me* for defending *you*."

"I'm sorry. I never intended to come between you."

"That's my problem to deal with. I stopped by to see how you are and if you need anything."

"I'm doing okay. I have a room, and a job, but then, you already know that."

Frankie looked beyond Spencer to the ship moored in the harbor. "What were you looking at just now?"

"That ship out there reportedly belongs to Makenna. I've been watching it for signs of life. So far, I've seen none. I'm beginning to wonder if it's been abandoned."

"Please be careful, Red. If what we've heard about her is true..."

"I *am* being careful, Frankie, but if she holds the key to who I am, I am willing to risk a little danger to find out."

Frankie looked at the clock on the bell tower across the docks. "I guess I should be going. I'm supposed to meet Lei for dinner at a local restaurant in about ten minutes." Frankie closed the distance between them and placed a gentle kiss on Spencer's cheek and then stepped back. "Please be careful," she whispered.

Spencer nodded. "I will. Oh, maybe I should give this back to you." Spencer unbuckled the gun belt around her waist.

"No. Keep it. I know where it is if I need it. I suspect you will need it more than I do right now."

"Thank you. Please tell Leilani I am sorry for injuring her, and that I will let you know if I learn anything about Makenna."

Frankie nodded. "It looks like we're going to be on O'ahu for a while, so I'll check in with you again in a few days. Be careful."

"I will." Spencer watched Frankie until she reached the end of the dock and walked out of sight. She sighed and turned back for one more look at the ship. Her breath caught in her throat as she realized there were lights shining from the portholes. She quickly fished the monocular from her pocket and extended it as far as it would go. "Well, I'll be damned. It's not abandoned after all."

***

Makenna paced back and forth across the captain's quarters. She waived her monocular telescope around as she spoke. "I want to know who he is!"

"But, Makenna..." First mate Roberts attempted to interject.

"Don't *'but Makenna'* me. Whoever that is has been watching us for three days." She thrust her telescope forward. "I've seen him with my own eyes, and he's not even trying to hide it."

"What harm is he doing?" Roberts questioned.

"What harm? Did you say, what harm? He has effectively paralyzed us. How can we do anything with him watching?"

"You don't know that he's watching us. He could be just scanning the horizon."

Makenna walked up to her first mate and leaned in close to his face. "Do I look like an idiot to you? Do I?"

"No, you don't."

"Then don't question me. Do you understand? I won't let anything stand in the way of our plans."

"He's been watching only during the daylight hours. If necessary, we'll execute our plans under the cover of darkness. It might be better that way," the first mate suggested.

"Are you out of your mind? How do you know he isn't watching at night as well...under the cover of darkness, I might add? No. Tomorrow, we find out who this bastard is, and why he's watching us."

"How do you propose we do that?"

"You're so fond of the cover of darkness. Use it to launch a skiff—tonight, and don't come back until we have answers. Is that clear?"

Chapter 16

Spencer made a point of being awake and on the dock before the sun rose the next morning. Breaking her routine, she spent the first hour of the day watching the ship in the harbor. At one point, Spencer heard a rustle in the bushes near the dock, but it was too dark to see, and since it only happened once, she brushed it off as being caused by wildlife.

Bear found her silently keeping watch just as the sun was beginning to rise.

"Good morning, Red."

Spencer extended her hand for a warm good morning handshake. "Same to you, Bear. Are you heading home for the day?"

"Soon. I wanted to let you know that some of the men saw lights on inside that ship last night. They went out around midnight."

"Yes, I saw them too. I watched for about an hour at dusk, but I wasn't able to make out any movement...just lights."

"No crime in lights, I suppose, but I thought you might like to keep an eye on it."

"I've been checking periodically throughout the day, and so far, nothing to report, but you'll be the first to know if something happens."

"All right then. Time to get some shut-eye. Oh, and before I forget, this is Friday, so you get the next two days off."

"Wow, you're right. I've lost track of time. Thanks for reminding me. I would have been standing right here by dawn tomorrow morning if you hadn't said something!"

"You're welcome. If I don't see you at the end of the shift, have a great weekend."

"You too! Sleep well, Bear."

Spencer scanned the area around the ship for a few more minutes, and then started her morning rounds of the warehouses.

***

Just before sunset, Spencer completed her final inspection. As part of her usual routine, she walked back to the far end of the dock and on the way, stopped to verify one final time that all the warehouse doors were latched and padlocked for the night. She then crossed the width of the dock and began her trek back to the far end while inspecting the vessels that were moored dockside. After four days on the job, she had become familiar with the boats and skiffs that were normally docked there. Occasionally, she would encounter a boat owner or two along the way, but on this evening, the dock was vacant and silent except for the sound of gentle waves washing up under the dock.

When she reached the end, she sat on the dock and retrieved the monocular telescope from her pocket to watch the ship.

For about an hour, Spencer scanned the ship and the area around it, but was disappointed when all remained dark and still. Finally, she climbed back to her feet and stretched her back. Then, as she turned to walk back to her room, she noticed a strange skiff she hadn't seen before, partially dragged ashore, just beyond the end of the dock. Curious, she descended the stairs to the beach level and approached the skiff. Her right hand was poised on the hilt of her sword as she walked.

The skiff was empty. Spencer relaxed and removed the telescope from her pocket to scan the shore and the area around the ship once more. After a moment or two, she was satisfied that all was quiet and she turned toward the stairs to the dock.

Suddenly, all went dark.

***

Makenna paced back and forth across the captain's quarters and anxiously awaited the return of the men she had sent ashore. Before long, she heard voices from the deck above.

"Haul it up!"

Makenna heard a loud thump on the side of the ship, following by more shouting.

"Take it easy, mate. We don't want to kill the lad. Not yet, anyway."

"This would be a lot easier if we lit a torch!"

"Can't do that. Orders from Makenna."

Makenna quickly made her way to the deck and watched her men in the dim moonlight as they winched a large burlap bag onto the deck and dropped it roughly to the floor.

"Take it to my quarters. I can't see a damned thing out here," Makenna instructed.

First mate Roberts ordered two men to heft the bag and carry it to the captain's quarters. Makenna went ahead of them to light a hurricane lamp. Again, they dropped the bag roughly to the floor.

"Remove the bag," Makenna demanded.

The men cut the rawhide ropes that held the bag closed and slowly pulled the bag off. Makenna watched intently as a pair of slim legs appeared, clad in leather pants and knee-high boots with buckles around the knee. The tip of a sword scabbard appeared next, followed by a sidearm.

"He's armed. Get that bag off so we can take care of that little issue," Makenna said.

The men quickly pulled the bag the rest of the way off.

Makenna took a quick step backward and then slowly approached and knelt beside their prisoner. She grabbed the lapels of Spencer's jacket and pulled her upward. Spencer's head fell back. There was a trail of dried blood streaked from Spencer's hairline, down the side of her face to her cheek. "In the name of Pele! It's a woman!" She looked at her men. "You morons ambushed a woman!"

She lowered Spencer back to the floor and stood up. "Unarm her, and then lock her in the brig. Roberts, you have some explaining to do!"

The men removed Spencer's sword from the sheath and the gun from the holster and handed them to Makenna. Then, they lifted her from the floor by her feet and underarms and carried her from the room.

Makenna turned to Roberts. "A woman. You kidnapped a woman."

"I know what it looks like, but she is the one who has been watching the ship. We saw her do it. We hid near the dock all day and watched. We would have taken her this morning before dawn, but one of the dockworkers approached just as we were about to jump her."

Makenna paced again. "Why would a woman be watching us?"

"I guess we'll have to ask her when she comes to."

Makenna picked up Spencer's sword from the table. "I wonder if she knows how to use this," she mumbled to herself. She turned back to Roberts. "See that she has food and water when she wakes up. And have the doc look at the wound on her head. Oh, and if any more harm comes to her, I will hold you personally responsible. Is that clear?"

***

Spencer rolled onto her back and moaned. Her body ached everywhere—especially her head. She reached up and ran a hand through her hair and encountered a crusty substance that she soon realized was blood. "What the hell happened to me?"

She forced herself into a seated position and looked around. She was in a small, dark room with a low ceiling, a door and one window with bars on it. Judging by the light coming in through the window, she guessed that it was mid-morning. Spencer did a quick inventory and realized her sword and gun were missing. *Great! No way to defend myself. Where the hell am I?*

Spencer crawled to the window and saw that she was on a ship. A crew member was nearby on the deck coiling rope. "Hey! Yes, you. Let me out of here," she called out. The crew member looked up and sneered, then walked away. She sat again and held her head between her hands.

Moments later, the door to her cell swung open and admitted a young man carrying a plate of food and drink. Another armed guard stood outside by the door as her food was being delivered.

"What the hell is happening here?" Spencer demanded.

The young man left and the guard closed and relocked the door.

"I said, what the hell is happening here?" Spencer repeated.

The guard looked in on her through the window. "Do yourself a favor and eat your food. The doc will be here soon to look at your head."

Spencer picked up the plate of food and threw it at the door. "I don't want your goddamned food. I want to get out of here," she yelled.

"Suit yourself," the guard said and then walked away.

Spencer screamed and then held her head in her hands once more in an attempt to stem the pounding in her temples.

Moments later, the door opened again, and Spencer looked up. Recognition was immediate.

"Doc? Doc, is that you?" Spencer scrambled to her feet.

Frankie walked into the room and motioned for the guard to close and lock the door behind her. "Yes, it's me," Frankie said.

Spencer wrapped herself around Frankie and wept. "I have never been so happy to see anyone in my life," she said. She stepped back and took Frankie's hands. "Did they kidnap you too?" she asked.

"Red, sit down and let me look at the wound on your head," Frankie said.

Spencer was clearly confused. "Sit down? You want me to sit down? Doc, we're being held hostage. Don't you realize that?"

Frankie pulled her hands from Spencer's grasp and led her to a chair. "I'm sorry, Red, but there are some things you don't know."

Spencer pulled away from Frankie and walked to the opposite side of the room. "Things I don't know? What are you talking about, Doc?"

Frankie once again approached her and tried to lead her back to the chair. "I need to look at your head wound, Red."

Spencer shook her off. "My name is not Red! It's Spencer!" she screamed. The shock on Spencer's face mirrored that on Frankie's as she realized what she had just said.

Frankie smiled and crossed her arms in front of her. "A memory has returned." She extended her hand to Spencer. "It's nice to meet you, Spencer."

Chapter 17

Makenna poured wine into two goblets and pushed one across the table. "How's our prisoner?" she asked.

Frankie picked up her wine and took a sip. "Confused."

"I guess if I woke up after being knocked out and kidnapped, I'd be confused as well," Makenna observed.

"It's a little more complicated than that," Frankie said.

"How so?"

"Lei and I have a bit of a history with her. You see, she was found washed up on shore at Princeville and she was brought to me for medical care. She suffered from a head injury and awoke with no memories of who she is. She was actually staying with us for the past few weeks."

"So why is she confused now...other than for obvious reasons?"

"It appears the little knock on the head your men administered when they kidnapped her, restored her memories...or at least some of them. We have been calling her Red for the past month. It turns out her name is Spencer."

Makenna stood up and carried her wine to one of the port holes. She gazed out across the ocean. "Do you have any idea why she was spying on us?" she asked.

Frankie did not respond for several long moments...long enough for Makenna to prompt her a second time.

"Frankie?"

Frankie sighed. "This is going to sound odd, but she thinks she's from the future."

Makenna's eyebrows raised high on her forehead. "The future?"

"Yes. Two thousand nineteen to be exact."

"So, she's not all there mentally?"

"There's more."

Makenna returned to the table and sat down. "I can't *wait* to hear this. What more can there be?"

"She has seen visions of you."

Makenna frowned. "Go on."

"She described your crescent moon tattoo to Lei and me in minute detail."

"I've never seen that woman in my life...and believe me, I'd remember her."

"Not in *this* life, anyway."

"Do you think she could be from the future, Frankie?"

"I don't know. You're the native. Your culture believes in the power and importance of ancestors and descendants. You tell me whether or not it's possible."

"So she was spying on us because she thinks she knows me?" Makenna asked.

"I believe she was hoping you could help her to restore her memories."

"So she wasn't spying on us for the government then."

"No, but then she's not ignorant about the unrest happening on the islands either."

"You'd have to be in a stupor not to realize what's happening on the islands," Makenna pointed out.

"Regrettably, Lei and I have been misleading her about your role in all of this."

"How so?"

"She knows you're a pirate...which technically, you are. And we've led her to believe you're part of the insurgency...which again, technically, you are. But what we haven't told her is that Lei and I are part of the insurgency as well. We felt we had to keep that from her so that the monarchy didn't discover they had..."

"Traitors in their ranks?" Makenna finished for her.

Frankie looked down at her hands, folded in her lap. "I don't feel like a traitor, Makenna. And neither does Lei. It is killing her to deceive her father, but we firmly believe the monarchy is wrong on this one. Hawai'i needs to be part of a bigger entity before some other hostile country forces themselves upon us. Of all the foreign governments out there, the United States is the best option. It is the one with democratic values that most closely match those of the kingdom. If we can get the monarchy to agree to the trade treaty, it will most likely lead to a more voluntary annexation of the islands."

Makenna finished her wine and put the mug down gently on the table. "Quite the mess we have created for ourselves here," she said. "So have you explained any of this deception to Spencer?"

"Not yet. I was hoping to have Lei by my side when I do that. In the meantime, she's still pretty confused."

"Is she dangerous? Dangerous enough to keep locked up?"

"Red wasn't dangerous, although she is an amazing swordswoman, but as far as Spencer is concerned...I don't know. I've just met her. Considering how gentle and kind Red was, I would suspect not."

Makenna reached for the sword and handgun Spencer had on her when she was kidnapped. "She was wearing these."

"The sword belongs to her, but the gun is mine. I lent it to her for protection when we reached O'ahu."

"Well then, you should have it back."

Frankie picked up the gun and walked to the door. She stopped and turned back around. "What are you going to do about Spencer?"

Makenna sighed heavily. "That's a good question. I guess for starters, I'd like to meet her and then judge for myself if she poses any danger to us or our mission. I certainly don't want to release her until she understands the full scope of what's going on here. That includes you and Lei clearing up the deception. But to ease your mind, Frankie, she is in no danger of harm unless she harms one of us first."

***

"Open the door."
The guard frowned at Frankie.

"I said, open the door. She's being moved to her own quarters."

"I haven't received any orders from the captain about that," the guard said.

Frankie crossed her arms. "I am here on Makenna's behalf. If you want to question that, I'll wait right here until you get back."

The guard hesitated.

"For Pele's sake! We are out to sea. Where do you think we're going to run to? Now open the damned door!"

The guard finally relented and removed the padlock from the door. Frankie threw it open and stepped inside. Spencer was curled up on the floor in the corner, holding her head.

"Red...I mean, Spencer, come with me. You're being moved to your own quarters."

Spencer looked at her. "Will I be locked up there as well?"

"No. You'll have free run of the ship. Now come with me."

Frankie helped her to her feet and steadied her when she almost fell from dizziness. Slowly, they walked out of the cell and into the sunshine. Spencer closed her eyes against the pain the bright sun caused inside her injured head.

"We don't have far to go." Frankie put an arm around Spencer and helped her up one set of steps to the upper level. Spencer held onto the railing while Frankie led her about ten yards to her quarters. The cabin was small, but clean. It had a full bed, a table and a chair. On the table were a washbasin and clean linens. On the front side of the cabin was a large window, and a door that also contained a window. Both allowed ample sunlight into the room.

Frankie led Spencer into the room and sat her on the edge of the bed. She helped Spencer to remove her jacket and vest, which she threw over the back of the chair. She then filled the basin with water and proceeded to clean the new wound on Spencer's head.

"Those goddamned gorillas," Frankie muttered. "I don't know why they felt they had to knock you unconscious."

"Because I would have kicked their asses," Spencer said.

Frankie grinned at her patient. "I think you could have, at that!"

Spencer reached up and grabbed Frankie's wrist to stop her progress. "Doc, what is happening here?"

Frankie shook her wrist free and resumed cleaning the wound on Spencer's head. "We'll save that discussion for later...when Lei is here with us."

Spencer brushed Frankie's hand away. "No, we'll discuss it now. Where is Leilani? Why are you here? Why are we out to sea and not moored in the harbor? What the hell is going on here?"

Frankie knelt on the floor in front of Spencer. "Spencer, I promise we'll explain everything to you, as soon as we get back to shore and Lei can join us. Please be patient. There is so much at stake here."

A tear fell from Spencer's eye and onto the hands she had folded in her lap. Frankie wiped it away and left a kiss in its wake.

"I'm sorry, Spencer. I am truly sorry. Please be patient. It will all become clear soon."

Spencer nodded.

Frankie rose to her feet once more and closely examined the gash on Spencer's head. "It looks worse than it is. I think the bleeding is under control. I can try to bandage it, but it might be better to leave it uncovered."

Spencer grabbed Frankie's wrist. "Doc, I need to see Makenna."

"And she wants to see you as well. In fact, I'm under orders to bring you to her as soon as you're ready."

"I'm ready now."   Spencer stood quickly, and immediately had to sit down again from light-headedness.

"Ah...no, you're not. Were you given anything to eat or drink since you've been on board?"

Spencer gave Frankie a crooked grin. "Yeah, but I threw it against the wall."

Frankie shook her head. "Well then, I need to get you something to eat. Wait here."

The moment Frankie left the cabin, Spencer was on her feet. She fought dizziness and nausea as she found handholds on the backs of the chair. Once she reached the door, she stepped outside and held onto the railing as she navigated the length of the ship. The cool breeze from the ocean made her feel significantly better as she pushed forward. Spencer had no idea where she was going, so she moved in the direction of voices she heard coming from the far end of the ship. Finally, she reached the door to the room the voices came from. She took a deep breath and pushed the door open. The occupants of the room froze.

The man inside the room immediately drew his sword. "How dare you enter the captain's quarters uninvited?"

"Roberts. Leave us," the woman said without breaking eye contact with Spencer.

Roberts hesitated.

"Now! And close the door on your way out," Makenna shouted.

Upon setting foot inside the room and through the entire encounter with Roberts, Spencer moved toward Makenna. She didn't stop until she was within a hair's breadth of her, all the while maintaining eye contact with her. Spencer lifted both hands and cupped Makenna's face between her palms. "Mak," she whispered before lowering her mouth to hers.

Makenna's world exploded around her. She could feel every cell in Spencer's being through that one small connection of their lips. Spencer completely took her breath away and replaced it with the essence of her own being. She welcomed the invasion of Spencer's tongue into her mouth and devoured all that Spencer was offering her through the intimate contact. She was no novice to sexual relationships with men and with women, but this was so much more. This was a connection of souls and a blending of hearts. This was not knowing where she ended and where Spencer began. This was trusting herself to become completely absorbed by another human soul.

The kiss ended and Makenna felt like her soul had been ripped from her body. She could barely move as her gaze locked with Spencer's.

"I've missed you, Mak," Spencer said before fainting away in Makenna's arms.

The door to the captain's quarters burst open. "Spencer!" Frankie shouted. "Damn you, woman."

"Frankie, help me get her to the bed."

"What happened?"

"She kissed me, and then fainted. I swear I didn't hurt her."

"She kissed you?" Frankie asked.

"Yes. Help me get her to the bed."

Together, Frankie and Makenna carried Spencer to Makenna's bed and laid her on her back.

"She hasn't had anything to eat or drink since she came on board yesterday," Frankie explained. "Help me to lift her head."

The two women worked together to revive Spencer just long enough for her to drink a little water before she passed out again.

"Will she be okay?" Makenna asked.

"She'll be fine as long as we can get water into her. I told her to stay in her cabin until I got back with food and water, but did she listen? No—of course not."

Frankie noticed Makenna's hand shaking when she reached up to tuck a stray strand of hair behind her ear. "Are you all right?"

Makenna was visibly shaken. "I don't know. Something happened when she kissed me. Something I have never experienced before. It was like, we were one person."

"*Aloha i ka'ike mua,*" Frankie said.

"Love at first sight? Do you think so?" Makenna asked. "Our elders teach us the concept of oversoul. Our oversoul contains all of the experiences we have gathered from previous lives. It comes to us in dreams, visions and even through intuition."

"Maybe your souls *have* touched in a different dimension. I mean, she *does* believe she's from the future," Frankie said.

Their attention was drawn to Spencer who rolled her head from side to side and then opened her eyes.

"Hey, there," Frankie said. "Here, let us lift your head. You need to drink some water."

Spencer stared at Makenna while they propped an additional pillow behind her head and held a cup to her lips for her to drink. "Thank you," she said.

"You scared us," Makenna said.

"The next time I tell you to stay put, I expect you to listen," Frankie scolded.

Spencer grinned. "I couldn't wait. I needed to see her." She looked at Makenna and then lifted her hand to touch Makenna's cheek.

Makenna shuddered. "Damn," she whispered softly.

Frankie felt like a voyeur. "So, Spencer, do you feel well enough to go back to your cabin?"

"No...no, she can stay here until she feels better," Makenna said quickly.

Frankie tried hard not to smile. "Are you sure? You'll need to keep feeding the water to her."

"I can do that. Really, it's no problem. I'll get her back to her cabin when she feels up to it," Makenna insisted.

Chapter 18

Roberts and Frankie were in the war room reviewing the schedule for their plan when Makenna came in.

Frankie looked up from the map that was spread out on the table. "How's Spencer?" she asked.

"She's sleeping. She went out as soon as you left. I'm a little concerned that she wasn't given food and water when she was locked up. I'll need to follow up on that."

"You don't need to do that, Makenna. Spencer confessed to me that she threw the food back at the guard when he gave it to her. It's her own damned fault that she's dehydrated."

"What are the two of you doing?" Makenna asked.

"Roberts and I were just discussing the schedule. I hope this thing with Spencer hasn't put us behind."

"It hasn't yet, but we need to talk about what to do with her. She is a variable I hadn't planned on."

"What do you mean?" Frankie asked.

Makenna didn't answer right away. Instead she walked around the room and then stopped to address Roberts. "Would you mind leaving us alone? I have something I need to discuss with the doctor in private."

Roberts frowned but then tipped his hat. "As you wish. I'll be at the helm if you need me."

Frankie watched the door close behind Roberts. "Makenna?" she said.

Makenna placed her palms on the map table and leaned forward. "I don't know what to do with Spencer. The way I see it, we can either keep her captive here, and maybe even recruit her for the cause, or we can put her back on shore and hope she doesn't say anything. I don't know if I can trust her. She's an unknown quantity. Hell, I don't even know how much she'll be missed if she doesn't go back ashore. That's the main reason we pulled out of the harbor last night. I didn't want anyone coming to look for her."

"She still doesn't know about Lei and me being part of the insurgency. Maybe we should tell her and give her the option to join us," Frankie suggested.

"And if she refuses?"

"Then we'll have no option but to keep her on board until it's over. We can't risk her exposing us to anyone. On the other hand, if she agrees to join us, there's a good possibility that she could be our eyes and ears on the docks if we put her back ashore."

Makenna nodded. "Okay. We'll head back into the harbor tonight. It should be dark in a few hours, so we'll slip into port after sunset. I'll run the red flag up the pole in the morning as a signal for Lei to come to the ship."

***

Makenna returned to her room to find Spencer sitting on the edge of the bed, pulling her boots on. She closed the door and leaned against it. "How are you feeling?" she asked.

"Tired, despite the fact that I've slept most of the day away."

"You've had a traumatic twenty-four hours. I'm sorry my men were so rough with you."

"Yeah, well, this whole month has been rough. I'll just put my boots on and get out of your way."

"You're not in my way, Spencer."

Spencer looked at her with sad eyes.

"You're breaking my heart with those puppy dog eyes. What's troubling you?" Makenna asked.

"I have this overwhelming feeling that my life has been turned upside down. I don't know who I am, and I absolutely know I don't belong here, but I'll be damned if I know my way home."

Makenna walked across the room and sat on the bed beside her. "You are Spencer. Frankie told me you recalled that name from your memory."

"Yes, my name is Spencer—but Spencer what? All I've got is a first name...and visions of you."

"You have visions of me?"

"Yes. You've come to me in my dreams. I know you, but yet I don't. The depth of emotion this woman in my dreams evokes is overwhelming. It *is* you...but yet it's not."

"How do you know it's me?"

"The woman who has appeared to me is beautiful...like you. She has the same face, same hair and same eyes, and she has a crescent moon tattoo above her left breast. She doesn't dress quite like a sexy pirate like you do, but it is definitely you."

Makenna pulled the corner of her left collar open. "A crescent moon tattoo...like this one?" she asked.

Spencer looked at the tattoo and wept. "Yes. Like that one." She reached forward and traced the tattoo on Makenna breast. "And in my dreams, it has a trail of stars leading down to..." Spencer's finger trailed over Makenna's clothing to where she imagined the trail of stars ended.

Makenna captured Spencer's hand and placed it inside her blouse. She closed her eyes and tried to control her own ragged breath as she released the two remaining buttons that held her breast captive. Her heart beat wildly in her chest as Spencer lifted her breast from inside her blouse and exposed the trail of stars.

Spencer looked directly into Makenna's eyes for silent affirmation, which she received with a perceptible nod of the head. Slowly, she lowered her face to Makenna's breast and inhaled the nipple into her mouth.

Makenna's head tilted backward, and she braced her arms behind her on the bed as a deep guttural moan erupted from her throat. "Spencer, by all that is sacred, I need more."

Spencer's head snapped up and she looked at the passion on Makenna's face. A vision flashed through her mind.

Shower stall...soap...tattoo...stars...Spencer, I need more! Mak!

Makenna opened her eyes. "Spencer. Please don't stop," she whispered.

Spencer rose from the bed and stood between Makenna's legs. She cupped Makenna's face between her palms and kissed her passionately, then placed a trail of kisses along her jaw line and neck. Makenna's head was once more tilted back and her eyes were closed. She leaned back on her hands.

"I've missed you, Mak," Spencer whispered.

Makenna's eyes flew open and she sat up. She pushed Spencer back. "What did you say?" she asked.

Spencer took a step back. "I'm sorry. Did I hurt you?"

Makenna reached out for Spencer's hand. "No. You didn't hurt me. You said something. What was it?"

Confusion clouded Spencer's features. "I don't remember."

Makenna inhaled deeply. "Spencer, I may not be who you think I am."

Spencer stepped forward and once again, took Makenna's face between her palms. "You are the woman from my dreams. I know how she makes me feel, and I know how *you* make me feel."

Makenna put her hands on Spencer's hips. "I don't want to hurt you, Spencer. You need to go into this with your eyes wide open."

"Eyes opened or closed, my heart sees clearly." Spencer kissed her tenderly. "Let me love, you, Makaya."

Makenna pulled back once more. "Spencer, you just called me Makaya."

Spencer's eyes opened wide and then narrowed into slits as she contemplated Makenna's words. "I did?"

"Yes, you did. Spencer, despite my reputation, this isn't something I take lightly. I can't be a stand-in for someone else."

"But you're not a stand-in. You're Mak. You're her...the woman who comes to me in my dreams. I swear you are."

"I *want* to be her, Spencer. Believe me I do. I have never met anyone who's had such an immediate impact on me like you do. The moment you walked into this room this morning, I felt like I had been struck by lightning. I literally couldn't breathe."

Spencer closed the distance between them one more time. She leaned toward Makenna, which caused her to lie back on the bed. Spencer hovered, supported by her hands on either side of Makenna's shoulders. Her nose brushed Makenna's cheek as she placed feather-light kisses on her lips. Her abdomen was pressed into the vee between Makenna's legs. "Let me love you, Mak," Spencer whispered hoarsely.

Try as she might, Makenna could not control the desire she felt for the woman above her. She wrapped her arms around Spencer and then slipped her hands into the waistband of her trousers. She dug her fingers into Spencer's buttocks and pulled her closer as she thrust her breasts forward and leaned her head back.

Spencer ground her abdomen into Makenna's core and nipped gently at her neck.

Makenna removed her hands and pushed gently at Spencer's chest. Spencer immediately suspended herself on her elbows and looked into Makenna's eyes. "Are you okay?" she asked.

Makenna tugged at Spencer's shirt. "Off with this. I want to feel your skin against mine."

Moments later, both had shed their clothing and they lay side by side on the bed, exploring one another's bodies. At one point, Spencer flipped Makenna and left a trail of nips and kisses from Makenna's neck, down her back and to the top of her buttocks.

Out of the blue, Spencer chuckled. "I remember these," she said.

Makenna raised her head and tried to look over her shoulder. "What are you looking at?"

Spencer grinned. "Your dimples. Here...and here." Spencer placed a gentle kiss on the indentation above each butt cheek. "I always loved those dimples," she added.

Makenna rolled onto her back and invited Spencer to lay beside her. "Come here." When Spencer complied, she traced her fingertips across Spencer's brow and down the side of her cheek. "Spencer, you've never seen those dimples before. This is the first time we've made love."

"Not true. I have made love to you countless times. I can't get enough of you, Mak. I want to make love to you through all eternity."

Spencer rolled on top of Makenna and kissed a trail from her neck to the triangle of hair above the center of her being...stopping at each breast along the way to nip and suck Makenna into a near frenzied state. By the time Spencer reached her final destination, Makenna was more than ready to receive her.

The climax was intense and emotional and at the peak of ecstasy, the concept of oversoul rushed into Makenna's mind, and she accepted that their souls were destined to meet and to be together again and again for all time and that perhaps...just perhaps, this was one of many encounters she and Spencer would make along the timeline of eternity.

Spencer climbed back up the length of Makenna's body and took Makenna into her arms as she cried. "I've got you, love. I've got you," Spencer whispered again and again until the emotions subsided and Makenna returned to herself.

Makenna traced Spencer's lips with her fingertips. "That was the most amazing thing I have ever experienced. Thank you."

Spencer smiled and kissed Makenna softly on the lips and then found herself on her back with Makenna straddling her hips.

"My turn to love you," Makenna said.

***

Leilani Kanhanamoku was in attendance at the morning session of the island council meetings when it was interrupted by a messenger.

"Forgive me for intruding, *Kaukau Ali'i*, but you asked me to inform you if the steam whaler returned to the harbor."

Leilani looked around the room. "Excuse me, *e na luna*." She rose from the table and followed the messenger out of the room.

"You say the ship has returned?"

"Yes, *Kaukau Ali'i*."

"Did it raise a flag?"

"A red flag."

"Thank you. You may go now."

Leilani returned to the meeting. "I'm afraid I must excuse myself from today's meetings, *e na luna*. Something has come up that I need to attend to. *Aloha*."

Leilani flagged down a passing carriage and went immediately to the port. As the carriage approached the docks, she saw the whaler moored offshore. Relief immediately flooded her senses, knowing that Frankie was on that ship. The ship had left its mooring the day before without warning, and she had hardly slept the night for worrying.

Leilani borrowed a skiff. Making sure she was unobserved, she surreptitiously rowed herself out to the ship. She tethered the small boat to the side of the ship and climbed the netting to the deck. Frankie was there to welcome her aboard.

The first thing Leilani did was to take Frankie into her arms and hold her close. Tears ran freely down Leilani's face. "By the gods, I missed you. I was so worried when I saw the ship had left. Please don't ever leave like that again without letting me know."

Frankie wrapped her arms around Leilani's waist. "Please don't cry, love. I'm okay. We're all okay. We had to leave unexpectedly. So much has happened in the past day. I have a lot to tell you, and we have more planning to do. Circumstances have changed."

Leilani held Frankie at an arm's length. "What is this all about, Frankie?"

"Come to our cabin and I'll tell you all about it. Then we need to meet the others in the war room to discuss what to do."

***

Leilani stood by the cabin door with her arms spread wide. "You're telling me that Red is on this ship? Are you seriously telling me that right now?"

"That's exactly what I'm telling you, but before you get all angry with her about it, you need to know that it's not her fault. She didn't come here willingly."

"Explain yourself."

"She was working as a security guard on the dock, and several times a day, she watched this ship through a telescope. Well, you know how Makenna is. It didn't take her long to notice the surveillance, and she sent some of the crew out to kidnap her. Now that she's here, we don't know what to do with her."

"Does she know *you're* here, Frankie?"

"Yes."

"Well that's just great!" Leilani said sarcastically.

"That couldn't be helped either. She was injured during the kidnapping and she needed medical attention."

"Lovely. So I assume she knows our whole plan then?"

"Not yet. That *is* an option, though."

"So what do we do now?"

"Makenna and I are at that point now. We don't know what to do with her. We're leaning toward telling her what's going on and hope she agrees it's the right thing to do, in which case, we could release her and recruit her to be our eyes and ears on the dock. The other option is to hold her hostage here until the whole thing is over."

"What does Makenna think of this?"

"Well, judging by the fact that Red didn't return to her cabin all night, I'd say Makenna wouldn't mind keeping her around."

"For the love of Pele, don't tell me they..."

"Yes, I do believe they have."

Leilani pointed to the door. "That woman has been nothing but trouble since she came into our lives!"

"Who are you talking about, Red or Makenna?"

"Both!"

"Oh, and by the way, Red's real name is Spencer. The knock on the head that Makenna's thugs gave her during the kidnapping shook that memory loose."

"Ahhhh!"

***

Spencer sat in a chair in the middle of the war room and waited for Frankie and Leilani to speak.

"Spencer, I'm sure you're wondering why we're having this meeting right now," Leilani said.

Spencer sat back and crossed one leg over the other. "Actually, no. I'm pretty sure I know why we're here."

Leilani raised her eyebrow. "Okay, so why don't you tell us."

"All of you are in cahoots with the insurgents. How close am I?" Spencer asked.

Leilani looked at Makenna. "I assume you told her all about it during your little pillow fest last night?"

Spencer lunged out of her chair and got into Leilani's face. "You have no idea what happened between us last night. Say what you want to me, but I won't have you disrespecting her. Am I making myself clear?"

Makenna walked in between Spencer and Leilani. "Stop. There's no need for saber rattling. Spencer, I don't need you to defend me. I can take care of myself. And Lei, I agree with Spencer—a little respect would be a good thing. There is a lot at stake here. We need to come to an agreement we can all support. Understood?"

Spencer sat down again and crossed her arms.

Leilani stood in front of Spencer. "I apologize. I shouldn't have been disrespectful. Like Makenna said, there is a lot at stake here. Let me try again.

"You are right. We are all involved in the insurgency. We believe Hawai'i is vulnerable, and in danger of being assimilated by one of many foreign governments. At this point, the offer on the table by the U.S. Government is an extension of the Reciprocity Treaty of eighteen seventy-five for seven more years in exchange for Pearl Harbor. At the end of those seven years, it would be an easy transition for the United States to just annex the Kingdom of Hawai'i.

"From where Frankie, Makenna and I sit, the Hawai'ian people have the best chance of maintaining our customs under U.S. rule than under the rule of any other foreign country in the area. For us, it's a win-win situation."

Spencer leaned forward in her seat. "Leilani, we had this discussion on the voyage between Kauai and O'ahu. If you remember right, I questioned why the monarchy was fighting it. To me, this treaty is a no-brainer. I agree with you. Why are we even having this discussion?"

Frankie stepped forward. "We are having this discussion because what we are planning to do could ultimately be considered treason, and in order to achieve statehood for Hawai'i *and* stay out of jail for the rest of our lives, we need the full cooperation of everyone involved."

"How does your father feel about this, Leilani? Didn't he send you to these island council meetings to try to *stop* an insurrection?" Spencer asked.

Leilani's shoulder's fell in defeat. "It haunts me every day, Spencer. Papa is from the old school. He believes Hawai'i will survive forever as a monarchy. I just don't see that happening. We are too small a nation. We have no military to speak of, other than what protection the U.S. provides. We would not survive a hostile military takeover from any country—including the United States. My thought is to more or less volunteer for a non-hostile annexation by the United States. I honestly think it's what's best for the Hawai'ian people...for my people."

"And what you're planning will accomplish that?" Spencer asked.

Makenna stepped forward. "What we're planning will make it near impossible for Hawai'i to survive without annexation."

"So what is this plan?" Spencer asked.

"Not so fast," Leilani said. "We can't tell you anything else unless we know you're in. In fact, we've told you too much already."

Spencer stood up and walked a few feet away. "Something doesn't feel right about this. This plan of yours was formulated long before I came along, so why involve me now?"

Frankie took Spencer by the shoulders. "To be honest, the fact that you're here at all complicates things. Spencer, we can't allow you to leave this ship if there's any chance you'll expose us to the authorities. Our only recourse is to give you a stake in the success or failure of this venture, or hold you hostage until it's through. I hate to put it that way, but that's the bottom line."

Spencer looked at Makenna. "Mak?"

"I'm, torn, Spencer. On one hand, holding you hostage definitely has it perks, but on the other hand, we sure could use your presence as an ally on the docks."

Spencer walked around the room, contemplating her options. "I can't tell *anyone* about this?"

"You can't tell a soul," Leilani confirmed.

"That's unfortunate, because the dock workers are all in favor of annexation. It's good for their business, if you know what I mean. They could be a huge help when the time comes."

Leilani shook her head. "Sorry, Spencer. You can't tell a living soul. If you can't commit to that, then the deal is off."

Chapter 19

On Monday morning, just before dawn, Spencer tied the gun holster to her thigh and strapped her sword to her hip before venturing out onto the docks to do her rounds. By the time she made it to the end of the dock, the sun was peeking over the horizon. She stood on the dock and looked at the ship moored in the harbor. The ship was positioned so that the captain's cabin was visible to her from where she stood. A rush of heat and emotion filled her as memories of lovemaking in that room filled her heart and mind.

The previous night, before they left the ship, Spencer had gone to the captain's quarters to say goodbye. As soon as she opened the door to the cabin, Makenna grabbed a handful of blouse and pulled her inside. She closed the door, pushed Spencer against it, and held her there with a searing kiss that she felt all the way to her toes.

Out of breath and fighting back tears, Spencer touched her forehead to Makenna's. "Promise me you'll be careful," she whispered.

"I will," Makenna choked out.

"Will I see you again before it happens?"

"I don't know. I need to leave tomorrow to collect the troops, but I'll be back in a few days. My heart hurts knowing you will be so far away."

Spencer pointed to Makenna's heart. "I will always be here."

Just then, Spencer heard Leilani's voice calling her. She looked over her shoulder toward the sound. "I have to go. Be careful, Mak. Please come back to me."

One more tender kiss, and Spencer let herself out of Makenna's cabin.

Leilani, Frankie and Spencer climbed aboard the skiff and rowed across the harbor late in the evening to attract as little attention to themselves as possible. Spencer slipped into her room at the docks after midnight and spent the rest of the night dreaming of a crescent moon and a trail of stars.

***

"Good Monday morning to you, Red!" Spencer was startled out of her reverie by the sound of Bear's voice.

Spencer turned around and shook Bear's hand. "Good morning. Sorry I jumped. You scared the living daylights out of me!

"You were pretty deep in thought there. It must have been a good weekend for you!" Bear winked at her.

Spencer had the decency to blush. "It was. And how was your weekend?"

"Pretty quiet. I didn't stray much from the docks. I noticed, however, that you were nowhere to be seen."

Spencer was both alarmed and annoyed that Bear was monitoring her whereabouts on her days off, but thought better of challenging him on it. "I stayed with some friends. Like you guessed, it was an enjoyable weekend." Again, Spencer blushed.

Bear slapped her on the back and laughed. "You're making this old man jealous, young lady!"

"How were things on the docks for the past two days?" Spencer asked out of curiosity.

"Nothing directly affecting the dock, but there seemed to be some activity around the ship in the harbor. Some comings and goings."

"Really?" Spencer was desperate to know if there was cause for alarm in his words.

"Yes. Nothing substantial, mind you...and of course, nothing illegal, but the ship sailed on Friday evening and returned later in the day on Saturday."

"Hmm. I wonder where it went?"

"No telling. But nothing illegal happened as far as I know. Rumor has it the people on that ship are part of the unrest we talked about a few days ago."

"Is that so?" Spencer hoped she sounded naively interested. "They're a sitting target out there in the harbor. If they were involved in the unrest, wouldn't the monarchy be doing something about it?"

Bear looked out at the ship. "There's no crime in sitting. So far, other than intimidating the authorities, nothing illegal has happened. I supposed they'll grow tired of it and move on at some point."

"You're probably right. In the meantime, I'll continue to monitor the situation for anything that appears strange," Spencer promised.

Bear put his hand on Spencer's shoulder. "I like you, Red. I'm glad you're part of our team. Well, I guess I should get something to eat followed by some shut-eye. You know where to find me if something out of the ordinary happens."

"That I do, Bear. Sweet dreams."

Spencer watched her foreman walk away, and then turned her attention once more to the ship in the harbor. By this time, daylight was in full bloom, so when Spencer lifted her telescope to her eye, she could clearly see the ship's details. She scanned the bow and then raised the eyeglass to look at the second deck. Her heart caught in her throat when she came eye to eye with Makenna looking back at her.

***

"*Kaukau Ali'i* Kanhanamoku, you have the ear of the people of Kauai. What are their feelings on the treaty?"

Leilani was distracted by the disruption in plans brought on by Spencer's interjection into the situation. The sound of her name forced her to back to awareness. "I'm sorry, could you repeat the question?"

"I asked how the people of Kauai feel about the treaty," the counselor from Molokai said.

"Counselor Mahelona, as you know—as we *all* know—this is not an issue about whether the people of Hawai'i agree with the treaty, or even wish to extend the treaty. I believe it is safe to say that both the kingdom and the United States have benefitted greatly from the past nine years of this relationship. No. This is really an issue about annexation, and I think the sooner we admit that and discuss it freely and openly, the sooner we can come to some agreement and a path forward."

Counselor Kekoa from Maui stood and slammed his hands on the table. "It is evident to me *Kaukau Ali'i* Kanhanamoku, that you are in favor of annexation. Does Chief Kanhanamoku agree with your position?"

"Counselor Kekoa, I am in favor of peace and prosperity for the people of Hawai'i. I expect that to be everyone's goal, who sits at this table. The unrest in this kingdom is anything but peaceful at this moment...and why, I ask you? Because this council is seriously considering ending the very thing that is making them prosperous. And to answer your second question Counselor Kekoa, my father also supports peace and prosperity, but like most of you at this table, he is unsure how to achieve that without giving up autonomy for the Kingdom of Hawai'i. I am sorry to put it this way, *e na luna*, but we may not be able to achieve both at the same time."

"But why not? Why can we not have both?" the counselor from Lanai asked.

"Because sir, we are vulnerable right now to attacks from outside forces. The way I see it, we can either leave ourselves open to a hostile takeover from a government, who may or may not respect our native ways...or we could voluntarily enter into a relationship with a nation who is open to at least our cultural autonomy, and to continue down the path to prosperity we have been following for a decade."

Counselor Hekekia from O'ahu rose to his feet. "One thing we have yet to consider is whether King Kalakaua would agree to a provisional government, because that will be a requirement if the Kingdom of Hawai'i is annexed by the United States, or any other foreign power for that matter. A provisional government will render him powerless." Counselor Hekekia walked slowly around the table as he spoke. "We have representation here from eight Hawai'ian nations, Niihau, Kauai, O'ahu, Lanai, Molokai, Maui, Kahoolawe and the big island of Hawai'i. In a show of hands who agrees that annexation would be good for the Kingdom of Hawai'i?"

All eight members of the council raised their hands.

"Now, who among us believe King Kalakaua will see the wisdom of this, and welcome annexation?"

Counselor Hekekia walked slowly to his seat and sat down. He looked across the table at the show of no hands. "You have your answer, ladies and gentlemen."

***

Spencer finished her first round of inspections by nine that morning. She took a break for a much needed breakfast of biscuits and ham, which she purchased at a local vendor on the docks. She carried her breakfast fare back to her room and sat at the table near the window to eat, keeping an eye on activities on the dock. While sitting there, she saw a familiar person pass by her window. "What the hell?" she whispered.

Spencer moved quickly to open the door and looked in the direction her passerby was headed. "Well, I'll be damned," she said. "He's normally sleeping by now."

Instead of returning to her breakfast, Spencer decided to follow him at a distance far enough not to be detected. He led her through a maze of buildings, until he finally disappeared into one of them.

Spencer crept forward, with her back against the wall of the building until she reached the door, which stood ajar to allow the early morning heat to escape the room.

"Will we wear something to cover our faces so we won't be recognized?" Spencer recognized Donovan's voice instantly.

"That's not a bad idea, Don." *Bear!*

"How about handkerchief?" another voice suggested.

"Also a good idea," Bear replied. "I also recommend we do not wear our normal dock clothes. We will still need our jobs after this is finished so we need to safeguard ourselves from being recognized."

"What about weapons?" *Donovan again.*

"No. This is supposed to be a non-lethal event."

"But what if they shoot at us first?" Donovan asked.

"None of you will be in the line of fire. Your job is to create a distraction—not to be directly involved. Is that clear?"

Spencer felt as though someone had punched her in the stomach. *Mak! That's Mak's voice!*

"Speaking of distractions, Makenna, how are we going to keep this from Red? She is obsessed with watching your ship whenever she gets the chance—especially after she spent the weekend on board with you."

A chorus of 'oohs' and 'ahhs' rang out from those in the room.

"That's enough," Makenna said good naturedly. "You leave her to me. I have plans for her."

Spencer felt sick. She stumbled away from the door and found an alley to throw up in. She washed her mouth with water from a rain barrel nearby and then leaned against the wall in the alley to compose herself.

Before long, she heard voices and watched quietly as the dock workers filed past her alley to return to their bunks. Bear was one of the last to pass by, but not before he stopped to talk to Makenna, close to where she was hiding.

"Sorry about the guys teasing you," Bear said.

"I've endured worse," Makenna replied.

"Just so you know, they like Red. She defeated Donovan soundly with her sword the day we met her. She fits in well with the crew. I just don't want you to think any less of her."

"Don't worry about it, Bear. She's my issue to deal with. Go on now. Get some sleep."

"Will do. Oh, James is waiting for you at the end of the dock. You'll need to leave soon or you'll be stuck here until after dark."

"Got it. Thanks."

Spencer watched Bear walk by and then waited with intentions of confronting Makenna. When Makenna didn't appear, Spencer realized she must have walked in the opposite direction. She was right. She stepped out of the alley in time to see Makenna turn the corner of the building. It didn't take long for her to catch up.

"Since when am I a problem you have to deal with?" Spencer said loudly.

Makenna froze.

"Since when, Mak?"

Makenna turned around. "It's not what it looked like, Spencer."

Spencer walked slowly toward her, with her hands held out to her sides for emphasis. "No? Tell me then—what the hell was that all about?"

Makenna looked down and ran a hand through her hair.

By this time, Spencer had closed the distance between them. She crossed her arms and leaned forward. "You lied to me, Mak."

Makenna's head snapped up. "I did not lie to you."

"Oh, yes you did. I asked you about recruiting the dock workers and you made me promise not to say anything to them. It turns out you already had them in your pocket. Oh...and it appears they know what happened between us as well. Did that mean *anything* to you, Mak? Did it?"

"I had to tell them, Spencer. They saw my crew kidnap you."

Spencer took a step away and threw up her hands. "Are you fucking kidding me? Has this entire thing been just a setup? Jesus Christ, Mak! I thought...I thought. Oh, hell, I don't know what I thought."

Makenna just stood there and shook her head.

Spencer put her hands on her hips. "You're not even going to defend yourself? Fuck this shit. I'm done!"

Spencer turned around and walked rapidly in the direction of her room.

"Spencer, stop. Spencer, please stop," Makenna yelled.

Spencer ignored her and continued to walk, which forced Makenna to run to catch up with her. Makenna grabbed her arm.

Spencer swung around and shook Makenna's hand off. "Don't you fucking touch me."

Makenna hauled back and slapped Spencer across the face.

"What the fuck!"

"Stop saying that! A little respect would be good here!" Makenna pointed out.

Spencer leaned into her face. "Who is disrespecting who?"

"We need to talk in private. Let's go to your room."

Spencer pushed the door to her room open and shoved Makenna inside. She closed and locked the door behind her.

"Can you please close the shutters as well?" Makenna asked.

"What's the matter? You don't want to be seen with me?" Spencer spat.

Makenna walked to the window and closed the shutters herself, casting the room into near darkness. "No, I don't want you to become a target."

"Why would I become a target?" Spencer asked.

"Guilt by association."

"What?"

"Spencer, I'm already under heavy suspicion. All I need to do is breathe wrong and I'll be locked up. Why do you think I've been staying on the ship as much as I have? I am being watched, and I don't need you to be targeted."

"But yet, you're here now."

"Yes. I am here now because Bear and his men give me cover. In fact, thanks to you, I've missed the ride back to the ship that Bear arranged for me."

"What are you talking about?"

"One of the local natives, a man named James, launches every day at this time to go fishing. No one would suspect he was carrying illegal cargo as long as he sticks to his routine. I'm afraid that is now a missed opportunity."

Spencer sat on the bed. "You wanted to talk in private, so talk."

"I don't want you to be involved in this insurrection."

"I thought my only choice was to be involved or to be held hostage on the ship. I'm wondering now whether being your concubine would have been a better idea."

"Don't say that, Spencer."

"Why not? Thanks to you, isn't that the impression the dock workers have of me now?"

Makenna approached Spencer and reached out to touch her face, but Spencer pulled back. Makenna dropped her hands to her sides. "I'm sorry, Spencer. I didn't want them to know you were involved. I didn't want you to become my weakness."

Spencer looked away. Even in the dimness of the room, the muscles in her jaw were visible as she clenched them in anger.

"Why don't you want me involved?"

"You don't have a stake in this, Spencer. You're obviously not from here. One day, you will go back to where you came from. I want you to have the freedom to do that. If you become involved in this insurrection, and if you're caught, you will go to jail for the rest of your life...or worse."

"And what about you?"

"That ship has already sailed. It's too late for me. If we manage to get away with this, I will be on the run for the rest of my life. I don't want that for you."

"I don't want to walk away from this, Mak. I know I'm just a *haole*. I know I'm an outsider, but *you* are involved, and so are Doc and Leilani. You three are my whole world right now and I won't desert my people."

"You complicate things for me, Spencer. I can't be fighting for the future of my people and focused on you at the same time. Please don't make me choose."

Spencer released a heavy sigh. "Does what we've shared mean anything to you, Mak? Do *I* mean anything to you?"

"More than you could possibly know. I may have only known you for a few days, but you will always be ingrained my mind and my heart. You've changed me in ways I can't yet even imagine, Spencer."

Spencer walked across the room and took Makenna by the shoulders. "I am angry with you right now. You ask me not to make you choose, but you expect *me* to choose, so choose, I will. I choose *you*. I choose *us*, and I will not walk away from that. You just need to deal with it."

"I can't deal with it, Spencer. I can't be responsible for ruining your life."

"That's bullshit and you know it. This is a decision I am making—not you. Tell me you really, in your heart of hearts, want me to walk away. Tell me."

Makenna's eyes filled with tears. "I can't."

"Neither can I."

Makenna touched the side of Spencer's face, and this time, Spencer did not pull away. "Make love to me," she whispered.

Chapter 20

Spencer completed her final inspection of the warehouses just before dusk. At the end of her rounds, she intentionally sought out Bear. He was busy unloading a ship that had just docked. She stood near the gangplank until he came out of the hold carrying two bags of grain. She made eye contact with him and nodded to convey the need to talk with him. She stood off to the side and waited for him to unload the two bags he was carrying.

"Is something wrong?" Bear asked.

"I need you to come with me. I need a skiff."

"You need a skiff? Like, right now?"

"Yes."

"You realize it's getting dark."

"Yes, I know. That's why I need it now."

He put his hands on his hips. "What the hell is going on, Red?"

She walked a few feet away and then turned around. "For starters, my real name is Spencer. You might as well start calling me that. So, are you coming with me or not?"

Bear called to his crew. "There's something Red needs help with. I'll be back soon."

Bear followed Spencer through the maze of buildings on the way to her room. When they arrived, Spencer reached for the handle and pushed the door open.

"Oh, Jesus," Bear said. "What are you still doing here?"

Makenna grinned sheepishly. "I got sidetracked." She cast a sly glance at Spencer.

Bear raised an eyebrow. "I bet you did." He looked at Spencer. "I'm not worried about you getting out to the ship, but will you be able to get back to shore in the dark?"

"I'll do my best," Spencer said.

"Or you can come back at dawn," Bear suggested.

"Or I could come back at dawn."

***

"Spencer. Spencer, wake up. It's time to go."

Spencer opened one eye and saw Makenna hovering above her. She reached up and pulled her down on top of her.

"Hey! Stop that! It's time to get up!" Makenna rolled off her and onto her back. Spencer followed.

"I don't want to go. I want to stay right here, naked with you," Spencer said.

"But I'm not naked. I've been up for an hour already. It's almost dawn. You need to get the skiff back in time for your shift to start on the docks. We don't need people questioning where you are."

"Ahhh! I hate it when you're right."

Spencer rolled off Makenna and stood to pull her trousers on.

Makenna climbed off the bed behind her and proceeded to tease her by pinching her nipples.

"Keep that up and this ship will not be leaving today to pick up the troops."

Makenna put her hands behind her. "You're no fun."

"There will be time for fun later." Spencer pulled her blouse over her head. "When will you be back?"

"Let's see. Today is Tuesday. It's two days there and two days back, plus a day to load supplies and discuss the final plans with the troops. I'm guessing I'll be back late on Saturday, or maybe on Sunday."

Spencer pulled on her boots and then took Makenna into her arms. "I'll miss you. Promise you'll be careful."

"Things will happen pretty quickly once we get back, Spencer. You need to be prepared for that."

Spencer tucked her shirt in and then grabbed her vest and coat. "I know. I won't deny I'm a little worried about it. In fact, I'm a *lot* worried about it."

Makenna handed Spencer's gun and sword to her. "Don't forget these."

"Thanks."

"Bear told me you're good with that sword."

"Yeah, I guess so. Something comes to me when I hold it."

"What do you mean?"

"I see things, and I remember things from before I came here. Doc has probably told you about where I come from."

"She says you believe you're from the future."

"Yes...a future that you are a part of."

"Ah, yes, the other me."

"You must think I'm crazy."

"Not at all. Pele sometimes works in mysterious ways. Oversouls can cross dimensions of time. My people believe souls can be connected through many generations. Maybe that is the case for us."

Spencer finished belting the sword to her side. "How do I look?"

"Like you just got out of bed after a night of passionate love making."

"Awesome! That's just the image I was shooting for."

Makenna cupped Spencer's face between her hands and kissed her tenderly. "I will see you in a few days."

"Be careful, and come back to me, okay?"

"I will."

***

"Doc! What are you doing here?" Spencer was surprised by Frankie while making her rounds.

"Lei is tied up in meetings again all day, but she asked me to stop by and invite you to have dinner with us. What time do you get off?"

"Usually at dusk, which at this time of year is around six. I can't believe it's almost December here. Where I come from, there is snow on the ground now."

"So that means, you lived somewhere in the upper part of the U.S. The southern parts don't have snow this early. I'm still guessing New England."

"I wish I could remember."

"Have any other memories returned other than your first name?"

"No memories, but definitely visions—especially when I handle my sword. This sword has something to do with who I am."

"So, are you interested in having dinner with us?"

"That would be awesome. I'd like that. I have a lot to talk with you about, although I suspect you already know more than I do."

"I'm of a mind that the more you understand going into this thing, the better it will go. I know Lei is frustrated about the lack of progress during the council meetings. I'm sure she'll want to discuss that."

"Okay, then. So we'll see you at our hotel around six?"

"I can't wait to have your *loco moco* again. I'll be there."

***

Spencer waited expectantly for Frankie to place a bowl of *loco moco* in front of her. "I've been waiting all day for this! I've bought this dish from some of the local vendors on the dock and nothing compares to yours."

Frankie blushed. "You give me too much credit."

"I agree with Spencer. You're an amazing cook, my love." Leilani picked up Frankie's hand and kissed the back of it.

Spencer smiled. "I love the relationship you two have. It warms my heart."

"Speaking of relationships, how is Makenna?" Frankie asked.

"I'm not so sure I'd call what we have a relationship," Spencer admitted. "One day, it seems like she's into me, and the next, she's more concerned about the insurgency than anything else."

"She has a lot on her mind. This has been a long time coming. The plans began more than a year ago," Leilani explained.

"I understand the goal here is to destabilize the kingdom, but to take this risk, there must be a huge payout as well," Spencer said.

"Yes, there will be a significant payout, but that is not why Makenna is involved. Her primary concern is for our people," Leilani explained. "There are a lot of moving parts in this plan, and a lot of people to compensate, so when it comes down to it, each share, although quite large, is still pretty modest when you consider what's at stake."

"So, what are your roles in this?" Spencer asked.

"My role is what I do best. I will be on hand to treat injuries, should they occur," Frankie said.

"How can they *not* occur?" Spencer asked incredulously. "I mean, based on what Mak described, a lot could go wrong, and this could turn into a bloodbath."

"We have reason to believe that won't happen," Leilani said. "For starters, they are unprepared for this, militarily. I mean, the King's Own guards have cannons that are not even assembled and guns with no ammunition. Sure, there are plenty of gun owners on the island, but none with the volume or power to resist something like this."

"You've mentioned before that Hawai'i has no real army to speak of. Doesn't the king realize how vulnerable the kingdom is?" Spencer asked.

"To be truthful, one reason these council meetings are so frustrating is because the king isn't even considering how vulnerable we are. He believes we are invincible and the only problem we face is the potential of losing our cultural autonomy. The only thing he remembers is the heyday of the monarchy and he truly believes there is no other way to govern this land. He isn't even considering that we could lose our entire kingdom if we are attached by a hostile power. The counselors are a group of old men who are afraid to cross the king, even though they know annexation is the right thing for our nation."

Frankie covered Leilani's hand with her own. "I'm sorry things aren't going as well as you'd like, love."

"Things will change dramatically in a few days," Leilani said. "As a people, I know we can get through this, but as a kingdom, I have little faith we can survive."

"In a few days?" Spencer asked. "It's happening that fast?"

"As soon as Makenna returns. Has she not explained the timeline to you?" Leilani asked.

"Actually, she's been pretty evasive about it. All she said is that things will happen quickly when she gets back. She didn't put an actual date on it."

"Fast is an understatement," Leilani said. "This thing is schedule for Monday, December first. That's a critical date based on the fact that the Pearl Harbor warships will be out to sea at that time."

Spencer sat back in her seat. "Why would she not tell me that?"

"What else has she been evasive about?" Frankie asked.

"To be truthful, she told me she didn't want me involved at all. She said it wasn't my fight."

Frankie smiled. "It appears Makenna is in love."

"What?" Spencer said.

"Has that topic not come up?" Frankie asked.

"No."

"Well, in my opinion, she doesn't want you involved because she's afraid she might lose you."

"You might be right, Frankie," Leilani said. "I've known Makenna since we were children, and she has never been evasive about anything. In fact, she's quite the opposite. How do you feel about her, Spencer?"

Spencer closed her eyes as a familiar phrase came to mind. She opened them and then looked at both her friends. "I am over the crescent moon in love with Makaya."

"Did you say, Mak... ow!" Leilani exclaimed. "You kicked me!" she said to Frankie.

"Sorry, my foot slipped." Frankie sent a meaningful look at Leilani. "So, Spencer, what is *your* role in all of this?"

"I don't know. She asked me to let her know if anything odd happens on the docks, but I found out yesterday that the dock workers are in on this too. They're supposed to create a diversion on the docks while everything else is going on. I was angry when I realized that. It felt like she didn't trust me with that information."

"Sweet girl,, she doesn't trust anyone right now. I think there are things she is even keeping from Lei and me," Frankie pointed out.

"Anyway, thanks to you two, I now know I have five days to plan my role in this."

"Spencer, I will caution you not to take too many chances—especially chances that may cause Makenna to lose focus. She is the glue that is holding this together," Leilani warned.

"So, where is Mak supposed to be when all of this is going down?" Spencer asked.

"She's supposed to be on the ship, preparing it for immediate departure as soon as it's over," Frankie said. "But I suspect she's not told us everything. I guess we'll find out on Monday."

Chapter 21

On Wednesday morning, Spencer intercepted Bear on his way to his room. "Bear!" She ran to catch up to him. "Bear, have you got a minute?"

"Good morning, Red. Yeah, I've got a few minutes. What's on your mind?"

"I want to talk to you about Monday."

A scowl fell over his face. "I don't know what you're talking about, Red. What's happening on Monday?"

Spencer crossed her arms. "You are a terrible liar, Bear. You know damned well what I'm talking about. Are you under orders not to talk to me about it?"

"You know what? I just remembered I don't have time to talk this morning. Sorry." Bear turned and walked away.

"What did you have planned as a diversion?" Spencer asked.

Bear stopped and turned around. He put his hands on his hips. "Damn you," he said. After another moment, he grabbed Spencer's forearm and dragged her toward his bunk. "We need to talk in private."

Bear opened the door to his room and pushed her inside. "Have a seat."

Spencer looked around his room as he retrieved two cups and a bottle of whiskey from the shelf. The room was larger than hers, and had considerably more amenities. It was relatively tidy, which Spencer did not expect from a man who seldom shaved.

Bear poured two cups of whiskey and slid one to her. He sat down opposite her at the table. "You weren't supposed to know about Monday," he said. "Makenna was unbending about that."

"I know what's going on, Bear. At least I know what she's told me. I am wondering now if she's been lying to me about those details as well."

Bear put his hand up. "Do yourself a favor and don't ask me for any of the details, because she hasn't given them to me. All I know is that the men and I need to start a diversion at the docks on Monday."

"Monday when? Monday morning...noon...night? Is it something I can help with?"

Bear picked up his whiskey and downed a large part of it before loudly putting his mug back on the table. "I can't tell you when...and no—it is not something you can help with. Even if it was, I'm under..."

"Strict orders not to tell me," Spencer finished for him. "I'm beginning to sense a pattern here."

"I'm sorry I can't tell you more."

"If even part of what she's told me is true, I'm not sure I'll be at work on Tuesday morning. In fact, I'm not sure there'll be a job to come back to after this goes down."

"Commerce will continue, regardless of what happens politically, Red. Unless things go horribly wrong, you will still have a job next Tuesday."

Spencer downed her entire whiskey in one gulp and then slammed her mug on the table. "Damn her!" she exclaimed. "I want to help. I want to do something that will make a difference, but I can't do that if all I'm told is mistruths."

"I don't know if this will make you feel any better, but when she told me to keep you in the dark, she said you meant too much to her for you to become complicit. She cares about you Red. It's her way of protecting you."

Spencer stood. "As you well know, I'm capable of taking care of myself. If she cared about me, she'd respect that I want to help. She isn't trying to protect me, Bear...she's trying to control me. Well, I'm here to tell you that *no one* controls me! Now if you'll excuse me, I have rounds to make. Thanks for talking to me."

Bear nodded and then watched as Spencer left his room and gently closed the door behind her.

***

At the end of her shift, Spencer entered one of the partially filled warehouses, lit a hurricane lamp for light and rigged several bags of sugar to hang on ropes from the rafters. These bags were spread out across a relatively large open area, and at various heights above the floor. This chore took several hours, at the end of which, she was covered in a sheen of sweat. She had long since shed her jacket and vest, and had opened her blouse nearly to her waist to cool herself down.

When Spencer was satisfied with the arrangement of the bags, she walked into the middle of them and drew her sword. She slipped her hand into the knuckle-bow and wrapped her fingers around the hilt. She pointed the tip of the sword toward the ceiling and held the blade a mere fraction of an inch in front of her nose. She closed her eyes and inhaled deeply.

Soon, a hazy vision appeared. Spencer felt like she was looking through a filter. She was in a large room, lit by powerful lights hanging just above her head...and she was not alone.

She and her opponent were both dressed in white one-piece suits, with white padded jackets and padded gloves. The tails of the jackets were held in place with a strap that passed under the crotch from the front and snapped to the jacket from behind. Knee-high, white compression socks and sports shoes completed the ensemble.

Spencer noticed that the one-piece body suit accentuated the supple curves of her opponent's rounded hips and full breasts. Her opponent had long dark hair pulled back into a ponytail. There was something familiar about this woman, and she longed to look into the face that was unfortunately covered by an oval-shaped mask with a black mesh face guard.

Spencer forced herself to take several deep breaths to calm her wildly beating heart. Suddenly, a buzzer sounded and she immediate stood on her mark. With her left hand raised at a ninety-degree angle, and her weight poised on her bent right knee, she held her sword pointed toward her opponent. A second buzzer set her into action.

Little did Spencer know, the flickering light of her hurricane lamp through the windows of the warehouse drew the attention of Bear and his crew. One by one, they made their way toward the warehouse door and stood mesmerized by the sight of Spencer's intricate swordsmanship as the bags of sugar posed as stand-ins for actual opponents. She weaved in and around the bags, striking blows, parrying, attacking, lunging and feinting. At one point, she did several back-flips across the room, landing on her feet with a striking blow to one of her opponents.

This went on for an hour until it became evident to the men that Spencer was beginning to tire. On Bear's signal, one by one, they returned to their work and left Spencer alone to finish her match.

Finally, exhausted, Spencer fell to the floor and lay on her back. Her chest heaved up and down until her breathing returned to a strong, but normal rhythm. The oil in the hurricane lamp dwindled and the light in the room dimmed.

Out of the corner of her eye, Spencer saw her opponent approach and kneel by her side. She felt her mask being removed and suddenly everything was clear again. Her gaze was drawn to the woman beside her as she shed her gloves and then removed her own mask.

Spencer wept. "Makaya," she whispered.

"I'm right here, love. It's all right. You're going to be all right."

Spencer's gaze darted around. Confusion was clearly evident on her face.

"Don't be afraid, my love. I am here for you. I love you with all my heart."

Spencer closed her eyes and whispered the name once more. "Makaya."

***

Leilani spooned herself behind Frankie and pulled her close. She buried her face in Frankie's hair and inhaled deeply. "I will never tire of your scent," she whispered.

Frankie rolled so that she was face to face with Leilani. "Nor I, yours, my love." Frankie traced Leilani's eyebrow with her fingertip. "I can't imagine living without you, Lei. I don't know what I would do if I suddenly couldn't remember our life together."

"You're thinking about Spencer?"

"Yes. I can't help it. I feel a bond with her. I don't know why."

Leilani grinned. "You have a way of picking up lost strays. Why should Spencer be any different?"

"I feel such a sense of helplessness in her. She is so out of her usual life. It's as if each day is a struggle to get through for her."

"Makenna isn't helping matters," Leilani pointed out.

"Lei, why do you think Makenna isn't being honest with her?"

"I think your observation was correct, Frankie. I think Makenna cares more for her than she'd like to admit and she's afraid of her getting hurt. That, and I don't think Makenna trusts her."

"Why wouldn't she trust her? She's like a lovesick puppy around Makenna. As far as I can tell, she hasn't done anything to give her reason to be mistrustful. On the other hand, *she* is the one giving Spencer reason not to trust *her*. I can't believe she's keeping the details of the schedule from her."

"Frankie, do you know if she's said anything to Makenna that might make her suspicious?"

"What do you mean?"

"Like yesterday when she slipped and said she was in love with Makaya? My shin is still sore from that slip up. Do you think she might have said Makaya's name in front of Makenna?"

"This is going to sound crazy, Lei, but I believe Makaya is real to Spencer. Whether Makenna and Makaya are the same person is what I don't know. I'm not even sure Spencer knows the difference between the two. She has said Makaya's name a few times now, but she seems to be unaware she's done it."

"I think keeping Spencer in the dark about certain things is not a bad idea. I mean, what if her memories come back at precisely the wrong time? That could be catastrophic for her...and for the cause. I think it's safer for her not to be in the thick of the action in the event something like that *does* happen."

"I can't help but worry that when Spencer's memories do come back, someone's heart will be broken. Maybe Makenna realizes that, and maybe she's already made the break before Spencer has the chance to," Frankie said.

"Or maybe Makenna realizes that she will need to disappear as soon as this thing is over, and if she can keep Spencer away from the action, she might be able to make her escape without a messy goodbye. I personally think she said her goodbyes two days ago."

"Would she leave just like that? Is she that heartless?" Frankie asked.

"I don't think she would see it as heartless, Frankie. I think she would see it as being compassionate to Spencer."

***

Spencer woke up near dawn and sat up. She was lying on the floor in unfamiliar surroundings. Her first instinct was to grab her sword and climb quickly to her feet. Upon doing so, she bumped into something, and swung her sword around quickly to defend herself. Her sword encountered something soft with a thud. The next thing she knew, something spilled from the object and gathered at her feet. *What the fuck?*

Spencer dropped to her knees and felt around. *Is this sand?*

Just then a beam of sunlight shone through a nearby window, and dimly illuminated the room she was in. She looked up and was startled to see several empty sugar bags hanging by ropes from the rafters. On the floor beneath each bag was a large pile of sugar.

She sat on the floor in this middle of it all, and held her head in her hands.

"You've got quite the mess to pick up." Bear's voice boomed from the doorway.

Spencer looked up. "What happened here?" she asked.

"You happened. Don't you remember?"

"I remember hanging the bags, but I certainly don't remember doing this." Spencer moved her arm in a sweeping motion to indicate the empty bags.

Bear walked across the room and reached down to help her to her feet. "The men and I saw the light on inside the warehouse, and when we came to investigate, we found you in the middle of some pretty intricate swordwork. I've never seen anything like it. It's a good thing those were bags of sugar and not people. Otherwise, I'd be calling the police force right now."

"I don't remember doing this. I woke up on the floor this morning. I must have spent the night here."

"I'm not surprised you don't remember. It was as if you were in a trance."

"I'm sorry. I'll clean it up right away."

"There's a shovel and a wheelbarrow in the shed at the end of the docks. I hate to do, it Red, but I'll have to dock your pay for the bags you destroyed."

Spencer nodded. "Yes, of course. I understand."

***

It took Spencer three hours to shovel up all the spilled sugar and to put the warehouse back in order again, after which, she executed her first round of inspections. After her rounds, she stood at the end of the dock and looked out into the harbor. It was empty of all ships, save several small skiffs with fisherman collecting their catch for the day. She felt a tremendous sense of loss and loneliness and fought back tears. "Come back to me, Makaya. Please come back," she whispered.

With a heavy heart, Spencer turned away and walked to her room, where she laid on the bed and stared at the ceiling.

I won't let you do this alone, Makaya. I will be there to protect you. I will die for you if I need to.

Fatigue brought on by emotion, quickly overcame Spencer and she promptly fell into a deep sleep.

Chapter 22

On Thursday afternoon, Frankie searched the dock for Spencer, to no avail. Just as she was about to give up, she ran into Bear. "Bear! I'm so glad to see you. Do you happen to know where Spencer is?"

"You mean, Red? I saw her complete her rounds a short time ago. Have you checked her room?"

"I'm not sure where that is."

"I can show you. Is everything all right?" he asked.

They walked slowly down the length of the dock.

"As good as they can be," Frankie replied. "I worry about Spencer's emotional state with all that is about to happen. I'm afraid Makenna hasn't been forthcoming to her about it."

"I know. She's been trying to get information out of me, but I'm under orders not to say anything to her. To be honest, the less she knows, the better off she'll be. If Makenna had her way, Red would be far away from here on Monday."

"Has Spencer told you anything about how she came to be here?" Frankie asked.

"No, she hasn't."

"She was found unconscious on Princeville beach in Kauai more than a month ago with a pretty severe head injury. She woke up with no memory of who she is, although some of that has been slowly coming back. Unfortunately, the injury has also left her with periodic blackouts."

"That might explain why she doesn't remember what happened last night."

Frankie frowned. "What happened?"

"I think she intended for it to be a practice session with her sword, but it turned out to be something else altogether."

"What do you mean?"

"She hung bags of sugar from the rafters, I assume to represent opponents. Some of us stood in the doorway to watch her. Her skill with a sword amazes me. It was like a dance when she began, but a few minutes into it, it seemed like she went into a trance. The men and I had to get back to work, so we didn't witness the whole thing, but when I checked on her this morning, she was kneeling on the floor in the middle of the warehouse, surrounded by empty bags hanging above her. They were empty because she had slashed the hell out of them and all of the contents spilled into piles on the floor. Funny thing is, she didn't remember doing it."

Frankie sighed. "I'm pretty sure there's some connection between her sword skills and the memories that are still eluding her. A couple of weeks ago, she had Lei pinned to the wall with the tip of her sword, but didn't remember doing it. I've seen the trance-like state firsthand."

"All the more reason to keep her out of the way on Monday," Bear said.

"I won't disagree with you, but I don't know how to stop her. She doesn't have all the details, but she knows enough to understand how dangerous this will be to everyone involved. She has convinced herself that Makenna is someone she was in love with before she came to us, and there is no way she will allow her go to into this without being there to protect her."

"Based on what I've seen, she'd definitely be able to take care of herself, and Makenna too, but if she gets into a mental state like she did last night, she could end up killing someone, which you know is the last thing any of us want."

Frankie nodded.

"Here's her room," Bear said. "If she's in there, try to encourage her to take it easy for the next few days. The dock will survive a day or two without her."

Frankie watched Bear walk away before she knocked on the door. "Spencer? Spencer, are you in there," she called. When no response came, she pushed the door open. The room was dark; too dark for Frankie to see adequately. She walked toward the window and opened the shutters. Daylight immediately flooded the room. Frankie heard Spencer before she saw her. She turned around quickly at the sound of whimpering behind her. Spencer was there—sitting on the floor in the corner—with her knees drawn into her chest, her arms hugging her legs and her forehead resting on her knees.

Frankie ran across the room and dropped to her knees in front of her friend. "Spencer. What happened?" Frankie quickly sat beside her and took Spencer into her arms. Spencer sunk down and laid her head in Frankie's lap. She shook violently. "Relax. You're safe. What happened, Spencer?" Frankie asked.

For several minutes, Spencer did not reply, but Frankie sensed the tremors subside. Finally, Spencer's breathing normalized to the point that Frankie thought she had fallen asleep. She leaned forward and noted that Spencer's eyes were open. She brushed the hair from Spencer's face. "That's better. Are you okay?" she asked.

Spencer wiped her nose with the back of her sleeve. "I feel like I'm losing my mind."

"What happened to cause this?"

Spencer sat up and leaned her back against the wall beside Frankie. She stared straight ahead. "I've been having visions. I don't know what's real and what isn't."

"Makaya?" Frankie asked.

Spencer looked at her. "Yes. She came to me last night. She said she loved me and would always be here for me. Doc, why is she lying to me?"

"You don't believe her?"

"How can I? She tells me she loves me and then she intentionally keeps the schedule from me, and she's telling people to lie to me as well."

"Who is she telling to lie to you?"

"Bear…and maybe you and Leilani."

Frankie reached and turned Spencer's face toward her by her chin. "Spencer, Lei and I have not lied to you. You can be sure of that."

"I don't know what I can be sure of. I feel like I'm standing on a cliff with one foot over the edge, Doc. I am terrified that this is as good as it will get."

Frankie took Spencer's hand. "Tell me about Makaya. Tell me everything you can remember about her."

Spencer smiled. "She is the most beautiful woman in the world. The intensity of love that I feel for her terrified me when we first met. I never believed in love at first sight until I saw her on the ship. I was drawn to her like a magnet. I know you told me to wait until you got back, but I had to see her." Spencer closed her eyes. "I remember I was in Hawai'i with her for a wedding, but I don't remember whose wedding it was. I know that she's a fencer, just like me. In my vision, she was my opponent. She came to me at the end of the match and removed her mask. It was *her* beautiful face hovering above me. She told me she loved me and would always be here for me. I want to believe her, but she's lied to me time and time again. She told me not to talk to Bear about the insurgence, and it turns out he's part of it. I don't know if I can trust her, Doc."

"So you and Makaya are sword fighters?" Frankie asked curiously.

"Yes, fencers. That's how we met."

"I guess that would explain why you're so good with a sword."

"That would make sense." Spencer looked at their clasped hands, and then back into Frankie's eyes. "I wonder why she became a pirate?"

"Makaya?"

"Yes. Maybe it pays better than nursing."

"That could be. I know being a village doctor has its rewards, but riches is not one of them."

Spencer squeezed Frankie's hand. "Today is Thursday, right?"

"Yes."

"Three more days before Makaya comes back. Then I intend to get some answers."

Frankie lifted their entwined hands and kissed the back of Spencer's. "Hey, why don't you come spend the next few days with Lei and me? There's no sense in you waiting here alone. It may even make the time go faster."

"I can't. I have to work," Spencer said.

"I ran into Bear this morning. He showed me where you room was, and before he left, he told me to encourage you to take a couple of days off. He knows how hard you've been working and he thinks you could use a break."

"Seriously?"

"Yes, seriously."

Spencer nodded. "Okay. Let me pack a few things and then we can go."

***

Frankie pushed the door to their hotel room open and encouraged Spencer to enter before her. "You can put your bag in the same room you stayed in before."

When Spencer emerged from the bedroom, Frankie turned. "Catch!" She said as she tossed a small pineapple to Spencer. "How does pineapple fried rice and glazed ham sound for dinner?"

Spencer grinned. "What, no *loco moco*?"

"Aren't you tired of that yet?"

"Not when you make it. In fact, I'll need your recipe. I think Makaya will like it too."

"*You* are going to cook?" Frankie teased.

"I can cook! Just because I haven't, doesn't mean I can't, you know. Oh, and for the record, pineapple fried rice and ham sounds yummy."

Spencer grabbed a knife and began shaving the rough outer layer from the pineapple while Frankie prepared the rice. "Will Leilani be late tonight?"

"Not too late. She has been trying to indirectly prepare the council for what is going to happen on Monday. That's not an easy task, considering she can't warn them in advance.

She is more or less trying to convince them that they should be developing a disaster recovery plan in the event *any* economic, political or natural disaster should occur. They're pretty set in their ways, so I don't know if they'll listen to her."

"What are you and Leilani going to do after Monday?"

"Our plan is to leave with Mak and then to go back to Kauai after a few days. As far as the council knows, we are leaving on Sunday. In reality, we will row out to the ship when it returns and stay there until after it's over. Chief Kanhanamoku believes we are going from here to Maui for a two-week vacation before returning home. Lei is hoping that by returning to Kauai after only a few days will convince her father that we came home early to help the monarchy deal with the catastrophe."

"Doc, I agree with what you are doing and why you're doing it, but I can clearly see why this would be considered treason."

"We are hoping the end justifies the means. Recovery under U.S. protection should be quick—especially with the new trade treaty to rely on."

"Where will Mak go after it's over?"

"That, you will have to ask her. Of course, there will be loose ends to tie immediately afterward, but once everything is settled, she can basically go where she wants."

"She told me that she'll be on the run for the rest of her life. That's one of the reasons she wanted me out of the picture."

"She told you that?" Frankie asked.

"Yes. She said I didn't deserve that kind of life."

"At least she was thinking of you first."

"Maybe. But then, I don't know if I believe her. And besides, if you love someone enough, you'd follow them to the ends of the earth—regardless of how hard it is. Wouldn't you do that for Leilani?"

"Without question."

"My point."

"Did I hear my name?" Leilani said as she walked through the front door.

"Hey, love. Welcome home," Frankie said. She met Leilani halfway across the room and kissed her tenderly.

Leilani looked over Frankie's shoulder. "Spencer! Nice to see you."

"Your lady invited me for dinner, for which, I am grateful," Spencer said.

Frankie returned to the stove to stir the rice. "Spencer's had a tough couple of days. I've invited her to stay for the weekend."

Leilani pulled a bottle of wine from the ice box and then retrieved three glasses from the cupboard. "Tough in what way?" she asked. "Is it something we can help with?"

"You already are by being good friends. My issues are more with Makaya. I'm tired of her lying to me and excluding me."

Leilani's eyebrows raised. "Makaya, huh? What is she up to now?" She shot a meaningful glance to Frankie.

"It's what she *isn't* up to. Specifically, she isn't up to telling me the truth about Monday, and I didn't even realize she was lying to me until I started asking questions of Bear."

Leilani handed a glass of wine to Frankie and carried Spencer's glass to her. She handed it to her and then clinked their glasses together. "Personally, I think you scare the shit out of her."

"Lei! Watch your mouth in front of our guest."

"I've heard our guest say much worse. Am I right, Spencer?"

"Damn fucking right you are!" Spencer replied, a wide grin on her face.

"See? So, like I was saying, I think you scare her. I think she cares for you and that realization terrifies her."

"That's no reason for her to lie to me...or to ask others to lie to me on her behalf."

"You're right about that. So, who else is lying to you?"

"Bear. I discovered that he has been in on this for quite a while now, and when I asked him about it, he said he was forbidden to talk to me about it. Under orders from Makaya."

"Makaya?"

"Yes. And then, she is so vague with me about the timing of all this. How can I possibly participate when I don't know where to be, or at what time to be there?"

"Frankie and I were discussing this last night, and we don't think she wants you to be involved."

"You are right about that. She told me the same thing in so many words...and Bear also said she implied that very thing to him."

"So, maybe you just say to hell with her and stay away all together. If she doesn't want your help, maybe you should shrug her off and what happens, happens."

"I wish it was that easy, Leilani. I wish it was, but I love her. I would die if something happened to her that I could have prevented. No, I need to be there, and I need you two to help me do that."

***

Frankie and Leilani lay side by side in bed that night. Neither was able to fall asleep.

"She believes Makaya and Makenna are the same person, doesn't she?" Leilani asked.

"She does. In fact, when I found her today, she was curled up on the floor in the corner of her room crying because Makaya had come to her in a vision the night before. She told me about it and then immediately went into a tirade about how Makaya, also Makenna, was lying to her about Monday. She seems horribly confused about both of them. First she told me she saw Makaya for the first time on the ship, then she told me they met because they are both swordswomen. She also wondered out loud if Makaya became a pirate because it pays better than nursing. Nursing? Can you see Makenna as a nurse? The amount of confusion and emotional pain she is in breaks my heart," Frankie explained.

"I've mentioned this before, Frankie, but do you think it's possible that she *is* from the future? I mean, what if all of this is some trick Pele has her caught up in and she was just thrust backward into *our* lives?"

"That seems like a pretty outrageous concept. I mean, if that was even possible, what would the chances be that she would be involved with someone who is an exact twin of Makaya? What would your ancestors say about this, Lei?"

"The Goddess Pele works in mysterious ways sometimes. In the Hawai'ian culture, it is conceivable that souls can cross generations in time."

"But in this case, it's not Spencer's *soul* that appears to have crossed over...it's her physical body as well."

Leilani rubbed her temples. "This is giving me a headache."

"I'm sorry, love. I wish I had an answer for all of this. Coming from a scientific and medical background, I have a hard time reconciling the metaphysical possibilities with reality. I just wish I knew how to help Spencer. Her confused vulnerability breaks my heart."

"So, how do we get out of this without lying to her, Frankie? Heaven knows, having someone else she trusts lie to her will only make things worse."

"I don't see how we *can* get out of it. And I agree—we can't lie to her. As much as Makenna might disapprove, I think we help her play a role in this."

Leilani nodded. "I hope we don't live to regret this."

Chapter 23

Spencer and Frankie spent Friday at the beach, longboarding while Leilani wrapped up her final day of meetings with the council. By mid-afternoon, they were beginning to tire and they carried their boards to the beach, spread out a blanket and sat in the sun.

Frankie glanced at Spencer. "You should probably put a shirt or a towel over your shoulders. You don't want that creamy skin of yours to burn."

Spencer draped a towel on her shoulders. "Thanks, Doc. It's a curse to have such fair skin. I burned so easily as a child, my parents should have bought stock in sunscreen."

"Sunscreen? What is that?"

Spencer looked quizzically at Frankie. It's an ointment that blocks the UV rays of the sun and protects skin from burning. Are you telling me sunscreen wasn't invented yet in the eighteen eighties?"

"I've never heard of it. UV?" Frankie admitted.

Spencer looked around at the people on the beach and chuckled. "It stands for Ultra Violet. Well, considering that the bathing suits women are wearing on this beach cover nearly all exposed skin, I guess it isn't required."

Frankie looked down at her own attire—a one piece suit with bloomers and puffy sleeves. "I think they're rather stylish."

"If you say so, Doc. I'm glad to wear these shorts and muscle shirt, even if I do look like a guy."

Frankie nodded. "Spencer, you mentioned your childhood. Do you remember much of it?"

Spencer was quiet for a few moments. "I can see snippets, like the sunscreen recall, but mostly it's a blank. Does this mean my memory is returning, Doc?"

"I think your memory is definitely returning, but apparently not all at once, and certainly not chronologically either."

Spencer gazed out across the ocean for a few minutes and then turned to Frankie. "Doc, I'm worried about what will happen when my full memory returns."

"What do you mean?"

"I'm concerned that I will finally know who I am and where I came from but that I won't be able to return to my own time. I mean, what if I'm stuck in the eighteen eighties?"

Frankie frowned. "I have to be honest with you, Spencer. I have my doubts that you really are from the future. Lei is more willing to entertain that concept, but I am struggling with it."

"I am from two thousand nineteen, Doc. I wouldn't lie about something like that."

Frankie stared into Spencer's face for a long time before she answered. "I believe you *think* you are from the future. I'm just having a hard time imagining it. Lei is more open to the idea, mostly because the Hawai'ian culture believes souls can travel through dimensions."

"Don't you have to be dead for your soul to travel through dimensions?"

"That's a good question. There are theories in the medical community that a person's soul can travel while in a psychological trance, but they are only theories. Nothing has been proven. Though the Hawai'ian culture believes souls can travel through dimensions, I believe that is only after a person dies. It would, however, make sense to me that you can't exist in more than one dimension at a time, so I would assume you'd have to cease to exist in one dimension in order to return to the other."

"So, are you saying I have to die in eighteen eighty-four before I can get back home to two thousand nineteen? That sucks!"

"I'm only speculating, Spencer. I don't know. You may not want to hear this, but you may have to resign yourself to living the rest of your life in this era."

Spencer's eyes filled with tears. "I can't do that, Doc. I can't leave Makaya...and I have other family as well. Did I tell you Makaya and I are engaged?"

"You are?"

"Yes. We were just beginning to start our lives together. I can't give up on that. That is why I need to help her with this battle on Monday. When it's over, we need to put this behind us and move on with our lives."

Frankie reached out for Spencer's hand. "Spencer, you *do* realize that Makenna is not Makaya."

"She *is* Makaya. I know it in my heart," Spencer replied.

"Hey, you two!"

Spencer and Frankie's attention was suddenly drawn to the sound of a familiar voice behind them.

"Lei!" Frankie exclaimed. She stood up and ran to her partner. Leilani embraced her warmly.

"Are you two having fun?" Leilani asked.

Frankie interlocked her arm with Leilani's and they walked back toward where Spencer was still sitting on the beach. "Yes, we're enjoying it very much. Spencer has taken to longboarding like she was born to it."

They were within earshot of Spencer by this time and Spencer reached up to take Leilani's hand and pull her down onto the blanket beside her.

"Is that true, Spencer?" Leilani asked.

"Where I'm from we call it surfing. It's not too different from water skiing. It's pretty much about balance and working the waves," Spencer replied

"Water skiing? What is that?" Leilani asked.

"Imagine two much smaller surfboards, I mean longboards strapped to your feet and a boat pulling you through the water. The thrust of the boat basically pulls you out of the water onto the skis and you glide along the top of the waves as the boat tows you around. It's a lot of fun...unless of course, you fall and face-plant."

"It sounds dangerous. Have you ever fallen?" Frankie asked.

"More times than I care to admit." No sooner had Spencer voiced these words, when a stabbing pain shot through her temples. She grabbed her head between her hands and cried out.

Frankie was on her knees in an instant. "Spencer? Are you all right?"

Spencer closed her eyes and pressed her palms into her temples until the pain subsided.

She could feel the wind blowing her hair around as she struggled to stabilize on top of the water. Finally, she leveled out and held onto the towrope with all her strength. *I've got this!*

She glanced now and then at the boat towing her, but was primarily focused on the waves and staying upright. Just as she relaxed and was enjoying her adventure, there before her was a large fin gliding through the water, directly in her path. *Is that a shark?* Before she could warn the occupants of the boat, her skis made contact with the creature, and she went down.

The pain in Spencer's head abruptly stopped and she looked at Frankie and Leilani. They were both kneeling beside her, wearing twin expressions of grave concern on their faces.

"Are you okay, Spencer?" Leilani asked.

"I...I think so," Spencer replied. "I saw a vision. I was water skiing. My skis made contact with a shark—or what I think was a shark."

"A shark? Are you serious? You're lucky he didn't attack you," Frankie said.

"Frankie, sharks rarely attack humans unless they're provoked," Leilani said. "The fact that she wasn't attacked most likely means the shark was an aumakua—a spiritual member of her family. Maybe it was her aumakua that helped her to the beach in Princeville."

Frankie felt Spencer's wrist. "Your pulse is returning to normal. How to do you feel?"

"I feel fine, Doc."

"Do you remember anything else?" Frankie asked.

"Only one thing—there were two people in the boat that was towing me. One was a woman with long, flowing black hair." Spencer closed her eyes again and focused on what she saw in her vision. She reopened her eyes and looked at Frankie. "The woman with the crescent moon tattoo. It was Makaya."

***

After dinner that evening, Spencer, Frankie and Leilani sat around a fire pit on the beach and enjoyed a glass of wine.

"Tell me about your day, my love," Frankie said to Leilani.

"There's not much to tell. I voiced my concerns one final time about how unprepared the islands are for dealing with major emergencies, and I recommended to the council that they seriously consider the offer from the Unites States to not only extend the trade treaty, but to become part of the union. Taking that one step would lead to continued economic prosperity, and would give the islands the protection we so desperately need from other hostile powers. I knew my recommendations were largely falling on deaf ears, but my position is now on the record. I also made it clear that I would be leaving the island on Sunday."

Spencer sipped her wine. "I know I've said this to you before, but if it makes you feel any better, Hawai'i was annexed by the United States in eighteen ninety-eight and then became a territory in nineteen hundreds and a state in nineteen fifty-nine. In my humble opinion, you did the right thing by taking the position you did, Leilani."

"Spencer, please don't say anything more. As I said to you a while ago, I don't think it is healthy for us to know the future...that is, given that you are *from* the future," Frankie said.

Spencer nodded. "I understand. I just wanted to confirm that Leilani took the right stance."

Leilani picked up the wine bottle and refilled all their glasses. "I'm not sure my personal stance will have much impact on the annexation of Hawai'i; however, I know that what we have planned for Monday will. There will be no way for Hawai'i to survive without annexation after that."

"When will Makaya be back?" Spencer asked.

"*Makenna* will be back no later than Sunday, but possibly even tomorrow if the organizers on the other end have prepared ahead of time," Leilani explained.

"Organizers on the other end?" Spencer questioned.

Leilani cocked her head to one side. "You don't think Makenna could pull this off by herself, do you? Of course there is outside help."

"Who?"

"I'm not at liberty to say. It may become obvious to you on Monday."

"Speaking of Monday, I need more details. I need to figure out what I can do to help," Spencer said.

"Frankie and I have been thinking about that," Leilani said. "And even though Makenna has made her feelings clear about leaving you out of it, we think your sword skills could go a long way toward making this successful."

"I know you and Frankie are planning to be out of the line of fire on Monday, but I suspect Makaya will put herself in danger on the front lines, even if she doesn't have to. Just in case, I want to be there to defend her in any way I can. I would never forgive myself if I just stood by and then something happened to her. Just point me in the right direction and I will be there to help."

Leilani leaned forward. "I have only one concern about your involvement, Spencer."

"And that is?" Spencer asked.

"I've seen what happens when you handle your sword. One of the fundamental rules of this engagement is that no one gets hurt unless it is in the act of self-defense. We cannot have you losing control while wielding your sword. If there is any chance of that happening, I will personally take steps to block you from participating. Is that clear?"

Spencer held eye contact with Leilani. "I will do my best, Leilani. I promise you that."

"Okay, so here's the plan..."

Chapter 24

On Saturday afternoon, Spencer, Frankie and Leilani made plans to shop in the open-air markets along the harbor. It was common for vendors to set up their wares near the docks for sale to tourists and other visitors who disembarked there.

Spencer was happy to find a pair of trousers and shirt that fit, and elected to bring them to her room on the docks instead of carrying them needlessly back to Frankie and Leilani's room. After depositing her purchases in her room, she began the trek back to the shopping area, when she noticed a crowd gathering near the docks. She went to investigate.

Spencer had to push her way through the crowd of onlookers until she reached the end of the dock. When she got there, she scanned the harbor for what was drawing so much attention. Her heart skipped a beat when she saw a large whaler making its way slowly toward the harbor. It was still a distance away, but Spencer knew in her heart who was on that ship.

"I was hoping to see the last of that thieving pirate!" someone said by her side.

Spencer wanted to respond to the man's comments, but she suddenly felt herself being pulled from the crowd. She was about to object when she realized the person who had a tight grasp on her upper arm was Bear. Spencer had little choice but to follow him to the other end of the dock.

"Bear, please let go of my arm. You're hurting me," Spencer complained.

Bear removed his hand from Spencer's arm.

"What the hell was that all about?" Spencer asked.

160

"We don't need you causing a stir, Red...or drawing attention in any way. I'm sorry if I was a little rough, but there's too much at stake here for you to ruin it with your temper."

"What makes you think I would ruin anything?"

Bear crossed his arms and raised his eyebrows at her.

"Okay! Okay, I confess I was ready to rip that guy a new asshole, but he pissed me off. Mak hasn't done anything to warrant those kinds of remarks."

"She hasn't done anything *here*, but her reputation does precede her, Red. She's not innocent, you know, and we don't need you giving anyone the impression that you are a pirate sympathizer."

"Spencer!"

Spencer turned at the sound of someone calling her name and saw Leilani walking toward them.

"Frankie told me you were taking your purchases to your room, so when I realized Makenna's ship was coming in, I thought I might still find you here."

"I want to see her, Leilani. Correction—I *need* to see her."

"I'm afraid that will have to wait. We can't risk you being seen with her. We can't risk *any* of us being seen with her. You'll just have to wait until all of this is over," Leilani explained.

"I agree," Bear said.

"And besides, she will drop anchor out by the reef and stay there for at least the next day. She won't move into the harbor until later. It will be too far for you to row out to...and you will draw too much attention to yourself if you try," Leilani explained.

"Why would she not come directly into the harbor?" Spencer asked.

"She can't risk anyone seeing what she has on board. She is beyond the reach of a telescope out there by the reef. I suspect it will be after dark before she drops anchor in the harbor. Now, Frankie is on her way to pick up a few produce items from the farmer's market. I told her we'd meet her there. She should be just about finished, so I need you to come with me."

Spencer turned to look toward the harbor. She felt the pained and heartsick expression on her own face.

Leilani squeezed her arm. "Monday is only two days away. Please be patient."

Spencer rubbed her forehead and then dropped her hands to her sides. "Okay. Okay, I'll try." She turned to Bear. "I will be back tomorrow evening so I'll be ready for work at dawn on Monday."

Bear glanced at Leilani and then at Spencer. "I think you shouldn't plan to come back to work until Tuesday. Things are going to get hectic around here on Monday."

"I agree with Bear," Leilani added. "Come on, Frankie is waiting."

***

Spencer went to bed that night in the guest room of Leilani and Frankie's suite. She lay there for hours, unable to get visions of Makaya from her mind. Finally, she got up and quietly made her way to the lanai where she sat in one of the chairs and lowered her head between her hands. She closed her eyes and thought about everything that had happened to her since she woke up on the beach in Princeville.

Slowly during the past month, some of her memories had filtered in. She remembered what Makaya looked like and her heart knew without a doubt, that Makenna was really Makaya.

She knew Makaya was as good with a sword as she was—and maybe better. Makaya had defeated her in their match in the warehouse. She knew Makaya was a nurse, but she struggled to understand why she had given up nursing to become a pirate. She knew that she was in Hawai'i for a wedding, but she couldn't remember whose wedding it was. She also knew that she and Makaya were engaged to be married. She distinctly remembered Makaya putting the flower behind her right ear when she asked her to marry her.

Spencer knew all of this, but she still didn't know who she was, and she didn't know where she came from.

The most important thing Spencer knew was that she was head over heels in love with Makaya. What she felt for Makaya went well beyond love. She *needed* Makaya in her life. She craved her touch, the softness of her skin, her intellect. She was the air she breathed, and she knew that she would surely die if something happened to her. This was the reason Spencer felt she needed to be there on Monday. She needed to be there to protect the woman she loved. She would die for her if necessary.

Spencer's head suddenly snapped up at the sound of a rustling noise nearby. She stood and looked around, but failed to see where the noise had come from. After a few moments, she relaxed and assumed it was caused by a bird. She turned around to go back into the room and then froze when a whisper called out her name. She whipped around quickly to see Makenna standing on the edge of the lanai.

Spencer's legs threatened mutiny and she held on to the chair to remain erect. "Mak!" she whispered.

Makenna rushed toward her and they embraced and clung to one another in desperation. "I have missed you so much," Makenna rasped.

Spencer took Makenna's face between her palms and kissed her soundly. She then touched her forehead to Makenna's. "Mak, is it safe for you to be here?"

"I couldn't stay away. We dropped anchor in the harbor about an hour ago, and I needed to see you. Bear told me where you were."

"Stay with me tonight."

"I don't have much time. I need to get back to the ship before daylight."

Spencer nodded. "We can make that happen. Please, stay with me through the night. I need to hold you."

"I will."

Spencer took Makenna's hand and quietly led her to her room. Once inside, she pushed Makenna up against the door and kissed her passionately.

"I need you, Spencer," Makenna said.

Spencer took a small step backward and removed Makenna's long leather jacket. She placed it on a nearby chair and unbuttoned Makenna's blouse as Makenna unbuckled the belt holding her sword and it dropped noisily to the floor. Spencer winced and looked toward the adjoining wall to Leilani and Frankie's room. She held a finger to her lips to indicate they needed to be quiet and then returned to her task of removing Makenna's clothing.

Spencer pushed the blouse from Makenna's shoulders and the leather trousers from her hips. She could barely control her trembling hands as they roamed across Makenna's back and buttocks. She grasped two handfuls of Makenna's backside and pulled her closer as she devoured her mouth.

"Make love to me, Spencer. I need to feel you," Makenna whispered.

Spencer took Makenna's hand and led her to the bed where she laid beside her and traced the outline of Makenna's naked hip with her fingertips. "You are so beautiful," she said.

Makenna tugged at Spencer's shirt. "Take this off."

Spencer pulled her shirt over her head, slipped her pants off and then lowered herself onto Makenna. Makenna spread her legs wide and allowed Spencer to lie between them. Spencer ground her abdomen into Makenna's core while placing tender kisses on her neck. "By all that is sacred, I love you, Mak," Spencer whispered.

Makenna's eyes flew open and she fought back tears, but she didn't respond.

Spencer shifted her weight to her knees and hovered above Makenna. She lowered her face to Makenna's and kissed her tenderly. Her tongue traced Makenna's lips before it dipped inside her mouth.

Makenna tilted her head to the side to allow Spencer better access to her throat. Spencer sucked on the sensitive skin of her neck and then moved to her breasts. Spencer teased Makenna mercilessly by spending an inordinate amount of time exploring the crescent moon tattoo above

Makenna's left breast with her tongue before she finally pulled the nipple into her mouth.

Makenna dug her fingers into Spencer's back and pulled her closer. "My God. That feels so good."

Spencer reached down and ran two fingers through Makenna's folds, and shuddered when she realized how wet she was. She tried to contain her own passion as she withdrew her hand and shifted her weight to hover above her. "I want to taste you, love," she said.

Makenna encouraged her to do just that. She placed her hands on Spencer's shoulders and gently applied pressure to guide her downward as Spencer slowly kissed her way down Makenna's body.

Spencer did not want to rush the time she had with Makenna. She resisted her effort to move forward quickly. She took her time feasting on Makenna's breasts and then slowly left a trail of nips and kisses down her stomach to her navel.

Makenna tried to push her lower. Spencer looked up at her. "Patience, my love," she whispered.

Spencer moved next to the area between Makenna's navel and hip. She ran her tongue in circles around her hip bone and then dipped into the crevice where her leg joined her abdomen.

Makenna's need grew too great to contain. She sat up and pushed Spencer to her knees. "Spencer, I need you, and I need you now!"

Spencer pushed Makenna back down onto the bed and lowered herself between her legs. For the next several minutes, she feasted on Makenna's essence.

Unable to control herself, Makenna moaned loudly as she raised her hips to meet Spencer's mouth.

When Spencer sensed Makenna was near climax, she drove three fingers deep inside her. Makenna arched her hips and met Spencer's thrusting rhythm. Before long, a low growl emerged from her throat and Spencer had to cover her mouth with her free hand to muffle the screams, as waves of orgasmic intensity flowed from the woman below her.

For a long time, Spencer savored the ripples of orgasmic spasms she felt running through Makenna until finally, they subsided and Makenna lay on the bed beside her like a rag doll. Spencer removed her fingers and gathered Makenna into her arms. She buried her face into the crook of Makenna's neck. "I will love you forever, Makaya," she said.

Makenna's eyes flew open and tears ran freely down her face.

***

Leilani sat up quickly in bed. "What was that?" she said.

Frankie rolled to her side and opened her eyes. "Lei, what is it?" she asked.

"I heard a noise. A clunking noise, like someone dropped something."

"I'm sure it's just your imagination. Come back to sleep."

"It wasn't my imagination, Frankie."

Leilani sat quietly in bed and strained to hear more. After several minutes, she gave up and lay down, but continued to listen. Frankie, in the meantime, went back to sleep.

Leilani forced herself to remain awake for as long as she could, but soon, she faded...that is, until a loud moan startled her awake again. She sat up and shook Frankie awake. "Frankie. Frankie, wake up."

"Lei, please. I'm tired."

"No. Wake up and listen."

Frankie sat up in bed beside Leilani and they both strained to listen in the darkness. It didn't take long for the muffled screams of passionate lovemaking to make themselves known.

***

Leilani sat in the dark common room and waited. Sometime before dawn, the door to Spencer's room opened and a lone figure exited. She watched the figure tiptoe slowly toward the front door and reach for the door handle.

"That was a pretty stupid move, Makenna."

Makenna jumped and she drew her sword.

"Put the sword away. You won't need it."

"Lei?" Makenna said tentatively.

"Yes."

"You scared the shit out of me."

"You are risking the mission by being here, Makenna."

"I needed to see her."

"You mean, you needed to fuck her. Yes...I heard you last night. You're playing with fire, Makenna."

Makenna walked toward Leilani's voice, and stopped just short of her. "No, I'm giving us both what we needed."

Leilani sighed audibly. "You know she wants to help on Monday."

"No! I don't want her anywhere near it," Makenna said vehemently.

"Why? Are you afraid for her...or do you feel that way for selfish reasons?"

"Selfish reason? What do you mean?"

"What I mean is that keeping her away will make it easier for you to leave. You have a way of avoiding commitment, Makenna. What happens to Spencer when you leave?"

"I am not who she thinks I am, Lei. She will survive—just like the rest of us. Now if you'll excuse me, I need to get back to the ship before daylight."

Chapter 25

After Makenna's departure in the early hours of Sunday morning, Leilani was too roused to sleep, so she made a pot of coffee and sat in the dark waiting for the rest of the household to rise.

Spencer was the first to emerge. Before sunrise, she threw open the door to her room and darted into the common area. She looked around frantically.

"She's gone," Leilani said from where she sat in the dark. "She's been gone for a few hours already."

"Lei?"

Leilani lit the oil lamp on the table beside her chair. The room was immediately illuminated by a soft yellow glow. Leilani tilted her head to the side when she saw Spencer. "Ah, you might want to put some clothing on before we have this discussion."

Spencer looked down at herself and realized she was naked. She abruptly turned around and went back into her room, only to reappear moments later with a robe on. "Sorry about that."

"Nothing to be sorry about—except, that is, the visitor you had last night."

Spencer put her hands on her hips. "I will never apologize for loving Mak," she said.

"Nor would I expect you to, however, having her here was a pretty reckless move on both your parts."

"I for one, am glad she came."

"I suppose you are," Leilani said. "I spoke with her before she left. She still insists that she doesn't want you involved with this event tomorrow."

"I don't care what she insists on. This is my choice, not hers," Spencer replied. "I want to know that she makes it through this unscathed, and I can help to make that happen."

"She won't like it one bit."

"What is she going to do about it...kill me?" Spencer quipped sarcastically.

Lei raised her eyebrows.

Spencer frowned. "You can't possibly think she'd do that, do you?"

"People have been motivated to do much worse for much less reward," Leilani said.

"I don't believe she'd ever harm me. She loves me."

"Does she, Spencer? Has she told you she loves you?"

Spencer sat back in her chair and sulked.

"I can see by the look on your face that she has never said those words to you."

"Makaya has told me repeatedly that she loves me," Spencer insisted.

"Makaya has...but has Makenna?"

"She loves me. I know she does," Spencer said pathetically.

"Spencer, we need to talk about what your plans are after tomorrow. As you know, Frankie and I are going back to Kauai sometime next week. In fact, we are packing up today and boarding Makenna's ship tonight. My father is going to need help holding the constitutional monarchy together until something is done to change that. As an only child, that responsibility will fall on me. You, on the other hand, have a job here. You will need to decide whether to keep it or to move on."

"I am going with Mak," Spencer said adamantly.

"Does she know that?"

Spencer stood and paced the room.

"Spencer?" Leilani prompted.

"We haven't talked about it, but that's what I want to do," Spencer said.

Leilani leaned forward in her chair. "Spencer, what do you think will happen when all of your memories return?"

"I don't know. I had this discussion with Doc. I simply don't know if I will suddenly return to the future, or stay here."

"I want you to know that you will always have a support network with Frankie and me. If you choose to return to Kauai, we will be there for you."

***

By mid-day on Sunday, November thirtieth, Leilani and Frankie were packed and ready to go. Leilani arranged with Bear to transport their luggage to Makenna's ship after dark.

While Frankie and Spencer stood on the dock waiting for Bear to collect their bags, Leilani went to the head of the Port Authority and recommended that a boat be sent out to the whaler to investigate the purpose of its return to the harbor. She volunteered her services as a representative of the Hawai'ian government, and suggested that Frankie go along in the event the purpose for their return was related to medical issues on board. It took little effort for Leilani to convince the authorities to carry out her suggestion, and by two that afternoon, she and Frankie were in a skiff and rowing toward Makenna's ship.

After a teary goodbye, Spencer retrieved her looking glass from her room and sat at the end of the dock to watch the ship. She was still there several hours later, after darkness had fallen.

Spencer was busy watching the ship when she suddenly felt a soft object hit her leg. Startled, she reached for the gun on her hip and drew it.

"Whoa there. Take it easy. There's no need to fire that thing. Now put it away before someone gets hurt."

Spencer looked up to see Bear standing beside her. "You scared me," she said.

"I thought that since you seem determined to sit here all night, that you might as well be warm, so I brought you a blanket."

Spencer holstered her gun and then looked down at the object that had hit her leg. She picked the blanket up and wrapped it around her shoulders. "Thanks, Bear. I appreciate it."

"Don't mention it. I'm about to take these bags out to the ship. Is there anything you'd like to send out with me?"

"Not unless you have a bag big enough for me to fit into," she said in all seriousness.

Bear squeezed her shoulder. "I know this is hard, Red. Hopefully, things will get better after tomorrow."

Spencer's chin quivered and she tried hard to hold it together. All she could manage without breaking down was a nod of the head.

"All right then. I'll be back soon." Bear picked up the two bags he had laid at his feet and descended to shore level where the skiff was waiting.

***

Spencer woke up the next morning with a stiff back. She rolled onto her back and opened her eyes, and to her surprise, all she saw was blue sky. She sat up abruptly and looked around. *Damn! I must have fallen asleep!*

After rubbing the sleep from her eyes, Spencer slowly climbed to her feet. She stretched the kinks out of her back and then immediately went in search of the commode that was located near her room.

The next stop was her quarters, where she washed and dressed in the new shirt and trousers she had purchased two days earlier, topped by her vest and leather coat. Feeling refreshed, she strapped on her sword and gun, and decided to get a bite to eat, after which she would make her normally scheduled rounds of the docks, despite Bear's insistence that she not return to work until Tuesday.

After her second set of rounds, Spencer returned to the end of the docks and sat to watch the ship through her looking glass. As usual, everything on the ship was dark. She could feel an odd sense of foreboding in the December air as the sun began its early descent in the western sky. Within a couple of hours, the sky would be dark, save the illumination from the moon. A great wave of sadness came over her as she watched the ship. Everyone who was important to her life at that moment was on that ship, yet, she was there on the dock, alone, and facing an uncertain future.

Spencer was suddenly startled by the sound of multiple conches sounding off. Within moments, men ran past her carrying buckets. "What's happening?" she asked.

"Fire! Either help or get out of the way!" one man yelled back.

Spencer was nearly knocked off the dock by several more men running toward the shore with buckets. She wisely decided to get out of the way and ran down the length of the dock to see where the fire was coming from. She reached the area of the dock containing the bunk houses and then turned the corner to the cargo landing. It was there that she noticed a large wooden cargo ship on fire.

She attempted to get closer for a better look, but was pushed back against one of the buildings by one of the dock workers.

"You need to get away from here," Bear said.

Spencer looked directly into Bear's eyes, and suddenly understood the silent message. *This is the diversion!* She nodded and ran the rest of the way down the dock and away from the shore until she reached the passenger launch. From there, she pulled her looking glass from her coat and scanned the ship once more. Expecting to see total darkness, this time, she saw lights emanating from every port hole.

It's happening. Think, Spencer! Think. Remember the plan. Spencer found a place near the dock to seclude herself without being viewed as suspicious, and then she waited. It would be two more hours before she would be needed. She waited and watched as countless dock workers and firemen ran back and forth between the ocean and the burning ship to pour ineffective buckets of water on ship that was now a raging inferno. Despite their efforts, the entire ship became engulfed in flames, and at one point, the heat from the fire was too much for those fighting, and they were forced to retreat and abandon it.

It was at this point...at ten p.m. on December first, eighteen eighty-four—when most of the town folk and nearly all of the law enforcement personnel in Honolulu were engaged in fighting the fire—that Spencer watched five boats loaded with armed men push off from the ship in the harbor and row directly toward the Oceanic Steamship Company's wharf.

From her strategic position, Spencer watched as natives fishing at the wharf ran into town to warn of the invasion. She scanned the first boat that landed for Makenna, but was sorely disappointed when it contained only men armed with the new Winchester repeating rifles, plus revolvers and cutlasses.

Spencer watched a man approach the first boat. He was unarmed, except for a notebook and writing implement.

"*Aloha*. My name is Thomas Brown, and I am a reporter for the Pacific Commercial Advertiser."

Before the man could say another word, the commander of the armed men stepped forward. "Grab him!" he bellowed. Immediately, the reporter was bound hand and foot. "Bring him to Nolte's coffee salon and hold him there, along with anyone else you encounter along the way," the commander instructed. "And remember—no casualties unless you are fired upon. Is that clear?"

From her hiding place, Spencer watched as each boat landed and the passengers disembarked. She counted no fewer than seventy men. It wasn't until the final boat that she saw the one person she hoped she *wouldn't* see—Makenna. *Leilani was right. She lied about staying on the ship.*

Chapter 26

Makenna jumped out of the boat and walked to the front of the gathering. She walked back and forth as she addressed the men.

"Gentlemen. We are here today as soldiers and as patriots. We are patriots for the Kingdom of Hawai'i and we are patriots for the United States of America. Unless provoked, anyone who kills or harms will suffer the same fate as their victim. This is not a coup. This is not a conquest. We leave here tonight with the spoils, but not at the expense of human life. Am I making myself clear?"

A chorus of "Yes, Commander," rang out.

"All right, then. Fall in."

Spencer watched as the armed men formed a single column and proceeded to march up Fort Street, led by Makenna and the commanding officer of the troops. Spencer followed closely behind, being careful not to expose her presence.

The streets of Honolulu were all but deserted on this night, partly because of the fire at the docks, and partly because of the late hour, so they were able to march forward relatively unimpeded.

The men marched up Fort Street directly to the Royal Hawai'ian Hotel. When they arrived, Makenna addressed the men. "The manager of this hotel, Mr. George Fassett, is a powerful citizen. We need to be ensured that he is unable to notify anyone of this raid. I want him silenced, but not harmed."

The commanding officer sent a half-dozen men into the hotel where they rounded up the guests and the manager and locked them in a room. One of the men was left to guard their prisoners while the rest of the unit moved on.

Spencer had the impression that the commanding officer was familiar with Honolulu as he ordered and led the troops to the next destination. She followed close behind by moving in and out of the shadows.

Just before they reached their next destination, Spencer made a dash from one alley to the next. She darted into the dark alley and was immediately taken off her feet by a blow to the stomach.

"Oh, my God," she moaned.

"What the hell are you doing here? Didn't I make it clear that I didn't want you involved in this? You could ruin everything. Damn you, Spencer!"

Spencer laid on the ground and held her stomach until the pain subsided. Then, she slowly climbed to her knees and sat back on her heels. "I can help," she said.

"You can help by going back to the docks!"

"You need my sword, Mak. I can help."

Makenna paced back and forth. "Do I have a choice now? Other than to kill you, that is?"

"I promise not to get in the way. Let me help."

"Ahh!" Makenna screamed quietly in frustration. She grabbed a handful of Spencer's jacket and pulled her to her feet. "One wrong move and I'll let the men loose on you. Do you understand?"

"Perfectly."

"You are to do what I tell you to do, when I tell you to do it. Nothing more...and nothing less."

"Got it."

It took a few minutes for them to catch up with the column of armed men. When they had made their way to the front, Makenna pushed Spencer in front of her and introduced her to the commanding officer. "John, this is Spencer. She's an extraordinary swordswoman. She will provide personal protection for you and me in the event we need it. She is to be unharmed. Do you have any questions?"

John eyed her warily through narrowed eyes. He leaned in close to Spencer. "I don't need a woman to protect me, but Makenna is the boss. Just stay out of the way of me and my men."

The troop of armed men continued to march directly from the hotel to the King's Palace.

Spencer walked beside Makenna. "Are you kidding me? You are going to invade the King's Palace?"

"He is having a dinner party tonight. He'll never suspect a thing," Makenna explained.

"Won't there be guards at the gate?"

"King Kalakaua has his own company of about forty soldiers called The King's Own; however, they generally do not guard the palace. They are most often used when the King travels, or in circumstances like this when the palace is under attack. There will be sentries at the gate, but no guard to speak of."

"Ah, hello? The palace *is* under attack, so shouldn't The King's Own be on guard?" Spencer asked.

"But the King doesn't *know* about the palace being under attack, so we are betting the guard will not be on duty."

"If they're not guarding the palace, then where will they be?"

"Probably in their barracks. There's the palace. Don't do anything stupid, Spencer, okay?"

The company of armed men marched directly up to the palace gates and overtook the sentries easily. Again, the sentries were bound hand and foot, and left with an armed guard. The rest of the troops marched directly to the palace doors.

"Kick the doors in," Makenna commanded.

John stepped up to the doors and with one hard kick, the doors flew open and slammed into the walls inside the room. Everyone in the room froze in place.

Makenna rushed into the room. "We are here as patriots of the Kingdom of Hawai'i," she proclaimed loudly. "Cooperate, and no one will be harmed. We are here to free the people of this island nation from monarchical rule. We are here to set the people and the government of Hawai'i on a path to greater prosperity and security. We have no intention of harming anyone unless provoked, or in self-defense. Commander, secure the room."

Spencer stood by and watched as the men gathered the guests together. Spencer also observed that a general had slipped past them through a rear exit. She immediately approached the commanding officer. "Sir, I just saw a general slip out that door." She pointed to the door on the far side of the room."

John quickly sent two men after him.

The Minister of Foreign Affairs stepped forward."Please, before anyone gets hurt, let's discuss this."

"Out of the way, Gibson." King Kalakaua pushed his way to the front. "I demand to know the meaning of this!"

Makenna stepped forward. "With all due respect, King Kalakaua, we have taken possession of the kingdom."

"For what reason?" he demanded.

"For foolhardy governing, Sir." Makenna said. "For putting the Hawai'ian people in danger of invasion by a hostile government, Sir. For not taking steps to secure the economic security of the Hawai'ian economy, Sir. Would you like me to continue, Sir?"

Out of the corner of her eye, Spencer saw Attorney General Neumann make a sudden movement toward Makenna. "How dare you speak to the king in that manner?" he yelled.

Spencer drew her sword and slipped the tip of it into the trigger guard of the gun Attorney General Neumann was pointing at Makenna, and with one smooth movement, flicked it out of his hand and sent it flying across the room. She then tripped him up so that he was lying on his back on the floor, and held him there by the point of her sword. "Don't move, and you won't get hurt," Spencer warned.

Makenna immediately ordered him bound. "Tie him up. Tie them all up!" she ordered.

"Including the king?" one of the men asked.

"Including the king. Lock them in the dining room and place an armed guard."

At this point, the two men sent to apprehend the general returned. They addressed the commanding officer. "Sir, General Hayley has alerted The King's Own and they are organizing a counterattack."

"Choose two dozen men and follow me to the barracks, Sergeant," John instructed.

"Commander," Makenna said. "Send word when all is secure so we can proceed."

"I'll go with them and report back," Spencer said.

Makenna nodded.

Spencer followed the troops through several twisted hallways until they located the barracks. As was reported, The King's Own was frantically trying to organize in order to beat down the rebellion. The commanding officer kicked open the door of the barracks and two dozen of his men filed in. Almost immediately The Kings Own lay down their weapons.

General Hayley was in the room with them. "What the hell are you doing?" he said to the king's men. "Shoot them!"

The captain of The King's Own shook his head. "We have weapons, but no ammunition. There is nothing we can do."

"Bind the general hand and foot and lock them all in the cellar." He approached the general and stopped within inches of his face. "You are damned lucky we are under orders not to harm, otherwise, you'd be a dead man right now." He looked at Spencer. "Go ahead and report back while we take care of these men."

***

All of the men not already assigned to guarding prisoners were assembled in the main hall. Makenna addressed them in a clear, crisp voice.

"First, let me congratulate you all on a job well done. So far, there have been no injuries. Let's keep it that way. Now that we have control of the kingdom, we need to execute step two of our plan.

"Commander, I need you to take about fifty of the remaining men and raid the following places." Makenna pulled a list from her jacket pocket and read from it. "First, the Treasury. You will need to enlist the help of the Public Registrar, Mr. Frank Pratt to open the vaults. Next, is the bank owned by Mr. C.R. Bishop on Merchant Street. After that, the business houses of W.G. Irwin & Co., G.W. Macfarlane & Co., Dillingham & Co., J.E Wiseman, Eisenberg & Co., C.O. Berger & Co., and the homes of Mr. W.G. Irwin, British Commissioner Major Wodehouse and the home of American Minister Mr. Daggett. The addresses to all of these are on this piece of paper." She handed the list to John.

"I hope I don't need to remind you gentlemen that no harm is to come to any of the people involved at these locations. When you have completed your mission, return directly to the ship with the spoils. We leave before dawn, so be sure to complete your tasks in a timely manner. Are there any questions?"

Makenna continued after no one spoke. "All right then. The remaining men will come with me. There are several valuable treasures right here in this palace that we will take ownership of."

Chapter 27

Makenna returned to the dock after her raid on the King's Palace, which yielded the sacred feather cloak of King Kamehamahas, a silver plate the king received as a gift on one of his European trips, a full silver service, and a number of other valuables. This, combined with the silver, gold and greenbacks taken from the treasury, business houses and bank raids was expected to yield more than two and a half million dollars.

Makenna approached Spencer as the men were loading the spoils into the boats. "I want to thank you for what you did back there."

"No need to thank me. That's why I wanted to be there. I would die if anything happened to you," Spencer said.

Makenna placed her hand on Spencer's arm. "Spencer, you don't even know me. Not really. We've only just met a few weeks ago."

"Not true. I have known you for more than a year. I fell in love with you from the start. Mak, we are engaged to be married."

"For the love of Pele, Spencer. Marriage is the furthest thing from my mind...even if it *was* legal—which it is not." Makenna ran a hand through her hair. "Spencer, I think we need to end this. As I've said before, I will be running from this for the rest of my life. That is no future for you."

Spencer shook her head. "I won't give up on us, Mak. I can't."

Their conversation was interrupted by one of the men loading the boats. "We're all loaded, Captain."

Makenna tried to covertly wipe a tear from the corner of her eye. "I'm sorry, Spencer. I need to go." She climbed into the nearest boat and sat with her back to the shore.

Spencer stood stoically as she watched the boat row away.

***

Spencer was still standing on the shore watching Makenna's boat row out of sight when the remaining men arrived with the spoils from raiding the financial houses.

"You're still here?" John asked.

Spencer had to think fast. "Yes, I am. I told Makenna I would stay to help you load the spoils."

John slapped Spencer on the back. "We welcome the help. By the way, good job there at the palace. That would have turned deadly if you hadn't been there to stop him."

"It's why I was there."

John turned to the men. "All right, let's get this loot loaded so we can get out of here before the news spreads."

For the next half hour, Spencer and the men transferred all of the loot from wagons to the boats. When they were finished, John looked around. "They should be here soon," he said.

Spencer didn't see anyone in particular. "Who are we waiting for?" she asked.

"The men we posted as guards for the prisoners. They are under order to release them unharmed and to return to the boats just about now."

No sooner had John said the words, than six men appeared a few hundred yards away, walking in the direction of the docks.

John waved them on. "Be speedy, lads. You are all that's between us and a good bottle of rum."

The six men broke into a run, and soon they...and Spencer...were seated in the boats and rowing toward the ship.

***

Makenna watched as the final bags of silver and gold were hoisted from the boats and onto the deck. A team of men were put in charge of moving the loot to a secure area of the hold while the others retrieved the rowboats from the water and secured them to the deck. She then turned to her first mate. "Mr. Roberts, weigh anchor and get us out of here!"

Makenna went to her cabin and stood at the window overlooking the shore. She had a pounding headache that she was sure was caused by the stress of carrying out this mission. She rubbed her temples as she watched the red glow on the docks caused by the still-burning ship. Soon, she noticed they were moving out of the harbor, and she released a sigh of relief that this part of the mission was completed without casualties.

A tear cascaded down Makenna's face when she realized this might be the last time she would ever see her beloved Hawai'i. She couldn't imagine a circumstance that might allow her to return after her treasonous acts. But she knew in her heart that it was the right thing to do for her island nation.

Makenna thought about Spencer, and felt an intense wave of anxiety pass through her chest. The pounding in her head increased, and she realized the anxiety bordered on regret. She had acknowledged to herself before the raid that she was in love with Spencer, but she refused to say it out loud. She refused to give Spencer hope that they had a future together. She was serious about spending the rest of her life on the run. She didn't want that for Spencer. She didn't want that for herself either, but there it was. There was no turning back.

Makenna lay on her bed and closed her eyes in the hopes that she could escape her heartache through sleep.

***

"Doc! Doc, are you in there?" Spencer waited on the deck in the hopes that Frankie would open the door before her presence was known.

Suddenly the door swung open. "Spencer? Spencer, what are you doing out there?"

"Can I come in?"

Frankie grabbed Spencer's arm and pulled her inside. "It's the middle of the night. What are you doing out there?"

"Mak doesn't know I'm on the ship."

"She what?" Frankie said in a loud enough voice to wake Leilani.

"Frankie? What's going on?" Leilani said sleepily.

"Spencer is here, and Makenna doesn't know she's on board."

Leilani sat up in bed. "Oh, great. How did you get on board without her knowing about it?"

"I went on the raid with her."

"Whoa...stop right there. You went on the raid with her?" Leilani asked.

"Yes. I was following them, and she caught me. It's a good thing I was there though, because someone tried to shoot her and I stopped him."

"So how did you get on the ship?" Frankie asked.

"I went back to the docks with her and some of the men after we raided the palace and she basically told me to get lost. She just rowed away without me. It turns out I was still there when the second group of men came back from the other part of the raid and they let me row out to the ship with them."

"Do you have any idea what pirates do to stowaways?" Leilani asked.

"Sure, they make them walk the plank."

"Exactly," Leilani confirmed.

"Wait! That's a real thing? I thought it only happened in pirate movies."

"Lei, Makenna wouldn't do that to Spencer, would she?" Frankie asked.

"Ordinarily, I would say no, but she might have to make an example of her in front of the men."

"So, what are my options?" Spencer asked.

"We could try to keep you hidden until she drops Frankie and me off at Kauai in a few days, or you could throw yourself at her mercy," Leilani suggested.

***

The next morning, Makenna scheduled a debriefing with Leilani and the commanding officer. "John. Come in. Let me introduce you to Leilani Kanhanamoku. Thank you for coming. Let me first say that I was impressed with your men. They handled themselves professionally."

"I would say the level of planning that went into this had a lot to do with it," John said.

"You can thank Lei for that," Makenna replied. "Her father is the chief of Kauai, and as such, she had access to some security information that we would not have had otherwise."

"I think we also need to credit Spencer," John added.

Leilani glanced nervously at Makenna.

"Spencer?"

"Yes. If she wasn't there, that minister would have killed you. That might have started quite a blood bath. Oh, and she's the one that noticed General Hayley had slipped away to the barracks. We were lucky to have her."

"Yes, of course. I'll have to remember to thank her when I see her again," Makenna said.

"I was also surprised to see how strong she was. She helped us load the loot into the boats and then onto the ship. She's definitely stronger than she looks."

Leilani visibly winced.

Makenna glanced at Leilani and then at John. "So, we are looking at a few days at sea and then a stop at Kauai to drop Lei and Frankie off. After that, we will deliver the goods to our contacts. At that time, you and your men will be paid, John."

"Why so many days at sea? Kauai can't be more than a day's sail from here," John said.

"That would be true if we were taking a direct route from O'ahu to Kauai, but we are not...for security reasons," Makenna explained.

"All right then. If there's nothing else, I will take my leave."

"That will be it for now, John. Thank you again for executing this flawlessly."

Makenna and Leilani watched John leave. As soon as he was out of earshot, Makenna slapped her hands down hard on the tabletop. "Tell me she is not on this ship."

"I think you know the answer to that already, Makenna."

"Damn her! This will ruin everything."

"And why is that?"

"I will need to change the entire schedule just to get rid of her."

"No, you don't. She will disembark with Frankie and me in Kauai and then you'll never have to set eyes on her again. In the meantime, we'll do our best to keep her away from you. Now if you're finished with me, I have plenty of other strategic work to do in my cabin to help my nation survive what we have just done to it."

Makenna waved her hand dismissively at Leilani, who promptly stormed out of the room.

***

Leilani returned to her room and slammed the door shut behind her. Frankie and Spencer both looked up from the game they were playing, with identical alarmed expressions on their faces.

"Ahh! That woman!" Leilani said.

"What happened?" Frankie asked.

"John happened."

"The guy who led the armed men?" Spencer asked.

"Yes. He was singing your praises at our debriefing about how you pitched in to load the loot into the boats and then to unload it onto the ship. He completely gave you up."

"Shit. So now what?" Spencer asked.

"Considering John believes you belong on this ship, she can't reverse course now and contradict that belief, so I think you're safe from the plank at least, but I think you should avoid her completely from now until we reach Kauai in a few days."

"I don't understand," Spencer said. "When she came to me Saturday night, she was so loving. She said she missed me. What could change so fast?"

"The Makenna on this ship is different from the Makenna you know on shore. Here on the ship, she has to be tough. She has to set an example for the crew in order to maintain control of them. She will be anything but loving in front of her men," Leilani explained. "*This* Makenna can be abusive and hard. *This* Makenna is responsible for the reputation she has. *This* Makenna is someone I would never associate with on a personal level."

"Why do I sense there is something else going on?" Frankie said.

"She just makes me angry when she doesn't appreciate the people around her. Spencer saved her life when they were at the palace, and how does she reward her for that? She abandons her—that's how. And then, she has the nerve to dismiss me like I'm some piece of trash! I am so angry I could kill right now!"

"She did that to you?" Spencer asked.

"Yes. I mean, I could understand it if some of her men were present, but it was just her and me in the cabin. There was no reason to treat me like that."

Spencer rose to her feet. "She can't get away with this." She took her jacket off and threw it over a chair and then walked toward the door.

"Spencer, where are you going?" Frankie asked.

"I'm going to set the record straight with her. I won't have her treating my family like that."

"Spencer, no!" Frankie yelled as Spencer stormed out of the cabin. "Lei, stop her!"

Spencer went directly to Makenna's cabin and pushed the door open. It was empty. "Makenna, where the fuck are you?" she yelled.

"Spencer, stop. This isn't the way to deal with her," Leilani warned. "She has an entire crew on this ship that will protect her. You can't take them all on."

"If she has any honor, she'll deal with me one on one. I just want to talk to her."

Spencer quickly made her way to the upper deck and stood in the middle of it. "Makenna, I am calling you out!" she shouted.

Makenna exited the pilot's cabin and stood on the upper deck looking down at Spencer. *Spencer, please don't do this. I don't want to hurt you.*

"What do you want, Spencer?"

"I need to talk to you, Mak. Preferably in private."

"Can't you see I'm in the middle of running my ship? I don't have time for this."

"Then make time."

"You don't know what you're doing, Spencer. Why don't you go back to your cabin and calm down?"

"No, I will not calm down. I'm tired of being treated this way."

"And what way is that?"

"You excluded me, Mak. I wanted so much to be a part of this. I wanted to support you. I wanted to protect you, and all you did was lie to me. If it wasn't for Frankie and Leilani, I would not have been there when you were almost killed last night. I risked my life to save yours and you rewarded me by breaking my heart. I love you, Mak. I would have died for you."

"I told you there was no future with me, Spencer. Life would not have been easy for you on the run."

"Don't you think that was *my* decision to make—not yours? What happened to the woman who came to me two nights ago? She was soft and tender. The person I see before me now is hard and unyielding."

Makenna made a gesture that encompassed the whole ship. "That woman does not exist outside of this world. Deal with it, or get off my ship."

"Why are you being such a bitch? You need to learn how to appreciate the people around you and to stop treating them like they are items you can throw away when they've outlived their usefulness."

By this time, a large number of crew had assembled to watch the exchange.

Frankie grabbed onto Leilani's arm. "Lei, please stop her."

Leilani approached Spencer and took her by the shoulders. She spoke in a voice only Spencer could hear. "Spencer, you need to stop this right now. You're pushing her to the point where she will have no choice but to fight you or lose face in front of her men. Please back down while you still have the chance."

"I'm not afraid of her, Leilani. I don't want to hurt her. I just want her to listen to me and to understand how she affects the people around her."

"You might be able to beat her, Spencer, but if you do, you'll have her entire crew to deal with, and there is no way you will win that battle. Please back down."

"I can't, Lei. I can't. Please understand."

Leilani lowered her chin to her chest and closed her eyes. When she opened them again she had tears flowing down her cheeks. She squeezed Spencer's shoulders. "Then win," she whispered.

Leilani walked away and Spencer turned her full attention to Makenna once more. "I just want to talk, Makaya."

A flash of anger crossed Makenna's face and she ran down the stairs toward Spencer. She stopped just inches from her face, placed her hands on Spencer's shoulders, and pushed hard enough to cause Spencer to fall onto her back. "I am *not* Makaya!" she screamed. "Get that through your thick head!"

Spencer was on her feet in an instant. She clenched her fists at her sides. "You're damned right about that. The Mak I know is tender and loving. You, on the other hand, can be hateful and cruel!"

"I'll show you cruel!" Makenna drew her sword and advanced on Spencer. Spencer barely had enough time to draw her own sword to deflect Makenna's attack.

Makenna's aggressiveness immediately forced Spencer into a defensive posture and she beat back Makenna's attack with a parry, followed immediately by a riposte. Makenna once more attacked by lunging while thrusting her sword forward, making contact with Spencer's sword. The force with which the blades clashed caused Spencer to stumble backward.

The crowd around them became agitated as the intensity of the sword fight increased. Shouts came from the men urging Makenna to kill her opponent.

Spencer tried to maintain eye contact with Makenna throughout the encounter, but time and time again, she had to focus her eyes on her sword and on any opening she could find to parry and counterattack. When she was successful looking into Makenna's eyes, what she saw there was bloodlust.

The encounter went on with frequent clashes of swords and near misses. At one point, their swords crossed near their hilts and it became a sheer battle of strength to break the deadlock...a battle won by Spencer, who violently shoved Makenna backward. They moved in choreographed motions across the deck as each took her anger and frustration out on the other.

In one final effort to end the confrontation, Makenna lunged forward and wildly swung her blade at Spencer. Spencer back-flipped away from Makenna and jumped onto a barrel that was situated near one of the railings, giving her a height advantage over her opponent. She executed a circle-parry followed by a counterattack and tore Makenna's sword from her hand, effectively disarming her. A split second later, Makenna was pinned against the railing by the point of Spencer's sword at her neck.

Spencer looked into Makenna's eyes and saw a faint glimmer of softness. "I don't want to hurt you, Mak."

"No!" Frankie screamed from across the deck. "Lei— stop him!"

A shot rang out just as Leilani tackled Roberts.

"Spencer!" Makenna yelled.

All eyes turned to the far end of the deck, in time to see Spencer topple over the railing and into the ocean below.

Leilani picked up Robert's gun from the deck and handed it to Frankie. "Shoot him if he moves!" A split second later, she dove over the side the ship and into the ocean, followed by Makenna and John.

***

"Where is she?" Makenna yelled. "Spencer!"

"Over here!" John called from several feet away. He resurfaced, holding Spencer under her arms. Her head was bleeding profusely.

As soon as their captain jumped overboard, the crew lowered the sails and brought the ship to a standstill as quickly as they could. Within minutes, they lowered one of the smaller boats over the side and rowed to where Makenna and the others were.

Makenna held on to the side of the boat. She watched them lift Spencer into the boat and lay her on the floor. "Be careful with her."

"We need to get her on board quickly. Frankie needs to look at her," Leilani urged.

It was a half hour before they returned to the boat and hefted Spencer onto the deck. Frankie was immediately by her side. Leilani knelt beside Frankie and Makenna on the other side of Spencer.

"Frankie?" Leilani said.

Frankie turned tear-filled eyes toward her partner. "I don't know if I can save her, Lei. She's lost a lot of blood."

Makenna picked Spencer's hand up and brought it to her lips. "Spencer, please open your eyes, love."

Spencer's eyelids flickered and slowly opened. The first person she saw was Frankie. She tried hard to smile.

Frankie kissed her on the forehead. She was unable to stop the flow of tears running down her cheeks, and several fell on Spencer's face when she kissed her.

Leilani took her hand. "Hey, tough guy." Her voice broke with emotion.

Spencer moved her head and looked at Makenna. "I am over the crescent moon in love with you," she said weakly.

Makenna sobbed. "I love you too, Spencer. I have right from the beginning."

Spencer smiled and closed her eyes. A moment later, she was gone.

Makenna spent the rest of the day and night watching over Spencer's body, still lying on the deck. She wouldn't allow anyone to touch her, except Frankie and Leilani. Together, they bathed her body and dressed her in clean clothes and prepared her for a burial at sea come dawn. Late in the evening, they sat on the deck and held hands, with Spencer between them. A great number of tears were shed for the woman they had only known for a short time.

Makenna sniffed loudly. "I will never forgive myself for treating her the way I did. We could have had a wonderful life together if I hadn't been so cruel to her. She was right. I was hateful. I wish more than anything that I could take it all back."

"We can only look forward, Makenna," Leilani said. "You need to learn how to forgive yourself and move on. Spencer would have wanted that for you."

Leilani turned to Frankie and wrapped an arm around her. Frankie lowered her head to Leilani's shoulder. She wiped her nose with the back of her sleeve. "In the entire time we knew her, she never once called me by my name. She called me Doc, and when I asked her to call me Frankie, she would just grin and call me Doc again. I pretended to be exasperated by that, but secretly, I found it endearing. What I wouldn't give to hear her call me Doc again."

"I believe we will see her again, Frankie," Leilani said. Leilani placed a hand flat on Spencer's stomach. "Please join me," she said to the others.

Leilani patiently waited while both Frankie and Makenna placed their hands atop hers. She closed her eyes. "The four of us are *ohana*, not because we share blood, but because we share a common sense of love and compassion. The ties that bind *ohana* cannot be broken by death. Our oversouls will touch one another again and again through the ages. It carries with it, all the memories from all our lifetimes. It is what allows us to recognize one another through countless lives. Goddess Pele, we call on you to protect our sister, Spencer and to grant her safe passage into her next life."

Leilani opened her eyes. "We will keep you in our hearts, Spencer, until we have the opportunity to be together again. *Aloha*, my sister."

Before long, each woman tired. They lay on the deck beside their friend and drifted off to sleep.

Frankie stood securely wrapped in Leilani's arms as they watched Spencer's body slide off the incline and into the ocean. Tears ran down both their faces and they said their final goodbyes to their friend.

Makenna stood at the railing, her knuckles white with the intensity of her grip. She kept her back to the others to hide her sorrow. She watched Spencer's body slide beneath the water and then closed her eyes and silently called on her aumakua to see her safely home. "Safe travels my love...until we meet again."

Chapter 28

Spencer felt like she was floating. Beneath her was total darkness. She rolled onto her back and was met with a brilliant light that appeared to be shining through a layer of water.

Where am I?

Held buoyant by her red life vest, Spencer floated along for quite some time. Sometimes her surroundings grew cold, and sometimes warm.

What has happened to me?

Spencer couldn't move her extremities. She was able to do little more than succumb to the movement of the water around her. After a time, she drifted off, only to awaken to the sun setting above her. The beauty of the sky ablaze in red and orange brought tears to her eyes.

This is so peaceful.

A sudden movement to her right caught her attention. She fought the water splashing into her face to see what was coming toward her. Soon, a shape emerged through the waves. It was a fin extending above the water.

Spencer couldn't look away, noting the fin growing larger as it approached. She felt a sense of excitement at the prospect that she was no longer alone. Oddly, she felt no fear.

Come closer.

Before long, she felt something bump her side. She tried to touch her new companion, but her arms would not obey. She tried to speak, but no sound came from her throat. She was caught in suspended animation. All she could do was watch.

Her companion swam under her until its fin gently made contact with her side. It pushed her along through the water, for several yards and then submerged and circled around again. It did this more times than Spencer could count.

Where are you taking me?

Before long, the sun set behind the horizon and the day turned to dusk, but still, her companion persisted. After a time, her companion suddenly stopped and surfaced close to her face. It hovered there for several moments, watching her. She looked into the one eye she could see and understood at that moment that it was sent to keep her safe.

Thank you my friend.

A sense of loneliness descended on her as her companion submerged for one final time and swam away. All alone again, she looked around in the bright light of the crescent moon and noticed the shore was but a few short feet away.

Thank you for seeing me safely home, aumakua.

***

Please come back to me, my love.

Spencer rolled her head to one side. She was aware of a distant voice talking to her.

I love you sweetheart.

Spencer frowned.

I miss seeing your beautiful green eyes. Spence, please open them for me.

Spencer's eyes flew open. She blinked a couple of times to focus her vision. There above her was a beautiful Hawai'ian woman with long dark hair and brown eyes. The woman was smiling broadly at her as tears rolled down her face.

"I have missed you so much, *ko'u aloha.* Welcome back." Makaya lowered her face to Spencer's and kissed her tenderly.

Spencer felt a jolting surge of desire with an intensity that took her by surprise. All Spencer could do was stare at her. Tears formed in pools at the corners of Spencer's eyes and spilled into her ears.

Makaya wiped away her tears and then cupped Spencer's face between her palms. "I see so much fear in your eyes, my love. Please don't worry. I will be here for you, no matter how long it takes."

Spencer felt tears well again and they spilled out onto her cheeks. Whoever this woman was, Spencer felt safe with her.

"Please don't cry, Spencer. Things will get better. I promise."

The woman wiped the tears from her eyes once more and then sat up. It was then that Spencer noticed something familiar. This woman had a crescent moon tattoo on her left breast, with a trail of stars that disappeared into her blouse. A phrase ran through Spencer's mind: *I am over the crescent moon in love with you.*

Spencer allowed an overwhelming feeling of love to fill her chest. She found it difficult to breathe, and she closed her eyes in an attempt to regain her composure. When she opened them again, suddenly, everything was clear.

"Makaya?" Spencer's voice was raspy and faint.

Makaya picked up Spencer's hand and placed it on her own cheek. "Yes, my love. You don't know how happy it makes me that you know who I am. I was so afraid you would be lost to me forever."

Spencer wept. "I love you, Mak."

"I love you too, Spence."

"W...where am I?" Spencer asked.

Makaya continued to hold Spencer's hand. "You're in the hospital on the island of O'ahu."

"What happened?"

"You were involved in a boating accident, love."

"I wasn't shot in the head?"

Makaya abruptly sat back. Her eyes opened wide. "For the love of Pele, why would you think that?"

Spencer became agitated. "We were on a pirate ship. We looted the treasury and while we were escaping, I got into a sword fight with you, and your first mate shot me."

Makaya placed both hands on Spencer's shoulders. "Sweetheart, there haven't been any pirates in Hawai'i since...since..."

"Since eighteen eighty-four," Spencer supplied.

"Yes, since eighteen eighty-four when the treasury was robbed and the economy of Hawai'i collapsed because of it."

"I was there, Mak. I was part of the raid, and you were too!"

"I was not...and neither were you. Spencer, you've been lying in this hospital bed in a coma for nearly six weeks."

"My body may have been here, but my soul was in eighteen eighty-four. I swear I was there, Mak. I swear it. And you were too. In fact, you were captain of a pirate ship."

"Spencer, do you hear yourself? *I* was a pirate? Really?"

"Yes, and I fell in love with you the moment I saw you. It was you, Mak. I could never feel this way about anyone else. It was you."

"So, how is our patient today?"

Spencer's attention was suddenly drawn to the doorway where the doctor had just come into the room. "Frankie!"

The doctor's head snapped up. "You're awake! That's marvelous!"

Makaya abruptly stood up from the side of the bed where she'd been sitting. "Wait a minute. Spencer, how do you know Doctor Wetmore's name when you've been in a coma this whole time?"

"I just know it. She was there too, and so was her partner, Leilani. Leilani helped to plan the raid."

Makaya walked a few feet away and then turned to face Spencer once more. Worry was clearly etched onto her brow.

"What am I missing here?" Dr. Wetmore asked.

"Spencer insists she traveled back to eighteen eighty-four and participated in a pirate raid, and apparently all of us were there as well...me, you, and Leilani."

A tall native woman who was passing by Spencer's door, abruptly stopped and looked in. "Did I just hear my name?"

"As a matter of fact, you did. Please come in," Dr. Wetmore said. "Spencer, this is..."

"Leilani Kanhanamoku. We've met," Spencer said.

Leilani looked confused. "It's true that as your case worker, I've stopped by to see you several times, but you've always been comatose. How is it you think you know me?"

"You were involved in the eighteen eighty-four raid on Honolulu. I was there with you," Spencer explained.

Leilani grinned. "You got one thing right...I do have an ancestor with the same name who helped plan that raid, but it surely wasn't me."

"But you look just like her. You and Frankie were partners. I lived with you while I was recovering. Your father was the chief of Kauai."

"One of my great grandfathers *was* the chief of Kauai. That is true. But again, it wasn't me. Heck, I'd be, what...one hundred sixty years old?"

Spencer struggled to raise her hands to her head. "I feel like I'm losing my mind."

Dr. Wetmore approached the bed and sat on the edge of it, facing Spencer. She extended her hands, palm up, to Spencer. "Give me your hands," she said.

Spencer haltingly lowered her hands and after two attempts, settled them in Dr. Wetmore's palms. "Not too bad. Now that you're awake, we'll need to add physical therapy to your daily routine. And while we're at it, we'll do a full psychological workup as well."

"You think I'm crazy, don't you?" Spencer asked.

"You sustained a pretty bad head injury when the water ski hit you. There is a mild amount of brain damage in that area. It would not be uncommon for there to be memory loss, or delusional fabrications, but I have confidence that the other parts of your brain will compensate and you'll make a full recovery."

"I am not delusional," Spencer insisted. "Leilani thought the same thing when I woke up in eighteen eighty-four and told them it was two thousand nineteen. If there's one thing I know for sure, I'm not delusional."

Dr. Wetmore reached for Spencer's chart on the wall near the door and recorded a few notes. "We'll schedule a full workup for you during the next day or two, but until then, feel free to push yourself physically."

Dr. Wetmore turned to leave, but stopped short and returned to Spencer's bedside. She leaned in close as if to examine her more closely, and whispered in Spencer's ear, "By the way, thank you for finally using my first name. The 'Doc' thing was getting old." She leaned back, winked at Spencer, and then left the room.

Epilogue

Frankie pushed the door open to her home and carried the groceries, through the entry way and into the kitchen

"Hey love, let me help you with those." Leilani met her halfway across the kitchen and took some of the bags from her.

"Thank you, Lei."

"How did the rest of your day go?" Lei asked.

"You mean, after Spencer woke up? Other than all the documents I needed to process on her, it went well. Now that's she's awake, the real fun begins."

Frankie put her bags on the countertop and then walked into the circle of Leilani's arms for a warm embrace. "Hmm, this feels good."

"That was a close call today in Spencer's room."

"Yes it was. I didn't expect her to remember the details so vividly after a head injury."

"I guess we made quite an impression on her," Lei remarked. "If you recall, she referred to us as her family when she was so angry with Makenna for disrespecting me after the raid."

"I feel bad for lying to her all those weeks."

"What do you mean?"

"I was so adamant about not believing she was from the future."

"Yeah, but at the time, you weren't aware that you were *also* from the future. You know as well as I do that our missions are subconsciously planted in our minds. We were as unaware of what was going to happen as Spencer was. It isn't until we returned to the present that we realized why we were there."

"I know, but it doesn't feel good *now*. She kind of grew on me when we were together, you know?"

"One thing I struggle with, Frankie, is about why there is so much secrecy around these missions. I mean, I understand not letting our subjects know what's going on, but why keep it secret from even *us*? As far as we knew, we were from the year eighteen eighty-four. Why do they use our subconscious minds to execute the plans?"

"I asked that question once. What I was told is that any time someone jumps into the past, their presence changes the space-time continuum. By doing it through our subconscious minds, they believe the impact will be minimal because we are programmed to focus on specific tasks rather than affecting random things that might change the future in a more global way."

"I guess that makes sense," Leilani said.

"Let me give you an example. Our mission this time was to assure the raid was successful without casualties. When the raid originally took place, many people were killed, including individuals who had the potential of benefitting our government. Our mission was *not* to stop the raid, or to broaden the scope of the raid...it was only to prevent people from dying. As you know, we were successful on that front—primarily thanks to Spencer. If Gibson had succeeded in killing Makenna, the outcome of the raid would have been different, and we would have failed in our mission."

"So, when we jump into the past, it has to be into the body of an ancestor, right?"

"Yes. That is correct," Frankie replied. "The ability to control the physical being our souls occupy when we jump is easiest when we share a bond with that person...specifically if that person is family."

"So, how is it that all our ancestors happened to be in the same place at the same time? I mean, the Leilani in eighteen eighty-four, was the chief's daughter, and Frankie in eighteen eighty-four was his doctor."

"And Makenna, who is Makaya's ancestor, was a pirate," Frankie added.

"What about Spencer? How did she end up in the middle of all of this?"

"I've been giving that some thought, and the only answer I can come up with, is that we are connected by the concept of *ohana*...our sense of family."

Lei shook her head as though to clear the confusion. "I don't understand."

"Here's what I think, Lei. When *we* were sent back on our mission, it was done under chemically induced comas and controlled conditions. That allowed the government to choose *where* and *when* we landed. Spencer, on the other hand, arrived on the scene because of a coma induced naturally through her boating accident. There were no controlled circumstances. There was no one directing where and when she would land. There was no programming of her subconscious mind. She knew she was from the future because that information wasn't programmed out of her like it was us. When she jumped, I don't think that's a coincidence that she landed with us. Just like it's not a coincidence that the four of us were in the same place today in Spencer's hospital room."

Leilani's eyes opened wide. "I am beginning to understand. On the ship, when Spencer died...we had the ceremony. I remember it word for word. *The four of us are* ohana, *not because we share blood, but because we share a common sense of love and compassion. The ties that bind* ohana *cannot be broken by death. Our oversouls will touch one another again and again through the ages. It carries with it, all the memories from all our lifetimes. It is what allows us to recognize one another through countless lives.*"

"Exactly," Frankie said. "When Spencer had her accident in two thousand nineteen, she almost died. While she was hovering between life and death, her oversoul sought out *ohana*, and it found all three of us in eighteen eighty-four. Our oversouls are destined to meet again and again throughout time. It is possible that eighteen eighty-four was the last time the four of us were together in the same place."

"So, what happens now?" Leilani asked.

"Right now, I'm going to make myself a coffee. Can I get one for you?" she asked.

"Yes, please."

Frankie opened the coffee maker and inserted a pod as she spoke. "As to what happens next...I have an update briefing with the company tomorrow to discuss Spencer's condition and to plan a covert interrogation. That is why I recommended a full psychological workup on her. I think we can learn a lot from her spontaneous jump experience...and of course, I want to make sure she gets the best care possible on the road to a full recovery."

"What did you think about Makaya?" Leilani asked.

"When I first saw her, I understood why Spencer thought she and Makenna were the same person. What freaks me out though, is that they *do* both have the same tattoo in the same exact location on their bodies," Frankie said.

"In the Hawai'ian culture, ancestral family is one of the most important parts of a person's history. It is not uncommon for traditions to be passed down from generation to generation—including tattoos. My mother had the same tattoo my grandmother had," Leilani said.

"But yet, *you* are a blank canvas," Frankie said.

"For now, anyway. Maybe someday I will carry on the tradition."

Frankie handed a mug of coffee to Leilani and then picked hers up from the countertop. She held it high before her in an invitation to toast. Leilani raised her own cup and they clinked the rims.

"To *ohana*," Frankie said. "May we always be together through countless lifetimes."

THE END

Photo Credit: Song of Myself Photography

See Karen's author page at www.karendbadger.com

About the Author

Karen D. Badger is the author of *On A Wing And A Prayer, Yesterday Once More* (a 2009 Golden Crown Literary Award winner for Speculative Fiction), *In A Family Way, Unchained Memories, Happy Campers, Collective Identity, Sweet Angel, and Relative-ly Speaking, Tailspin* and *Flashpoint* (Books I, II, III, IV, V, VI, VII and VIII of the Commitment Series), *The Blue Feather, All My Tomorrows* (sequel to the 2009 award winning *Yesterday Once More*), *1140 Rue Royale* (a 2017 Golden Crown Literary Award winner for Paranormal Fiction) and *Over The Crescent Moon*, her most recent release. All of these works have been released by Badger Bliss Books, which Karen co-owns with her wife Barbara Sawyer (aka Bliss).

Born and raised in Vermont, Karen is the second of five children raised by a fiercely independent mother, who remains one of her best friends. Karen earned her B.A. in 1978 in Theater and in Elementary Education, and in 1994, earned a B.S. in mathematics. In addition to her novels, Karen is the author of more than two dozen technical papers and journal articles on photomask manufacturing, which she has published and has presented at numerous semiconductor industry conferences and is the holder of several technical patents. Karen is currently in her 41th year as a Principle Member of the Technical Staff with a prominent semiconductor manufacturer in Vermont.

Karen and her wife, Barb (a retired Lt. Col., U.S. Air Force) live in the beautiful state of Vermont—home of Ben and Jerry's. They spend their spare time with family as well as doing home improvement projects on both their homes in Vermont and New Mexico. They also enjoy camping, kayaking, motorcycling and singing Karaoke.

Please take a moment to visit Karen's author website at www.karendbadger.com, or the Badger Bliss Books website at www.badgerblissbooks.com. Also like us on Facebook!

TITLES BY KAREN D. BADGER
www.badgerblissbooks.com

On A Wing and A Prayer
First edition published by Blue Feather Books, Sept, 2005
Second edition published by Badger Bliss Books, Sept, 2014
Third edition published by Badger Bliss Books, August, 2016
ISBN 13: 978-1-945761-01-0, ISBN 10: 1-945761-01-6

Yesterday Once More
First edition published by Blue Feather Books, July, 2008
Second edition published by Badger Bliss Books ,Sept, 2014
Third edition published by Badger Bliss Books, August, 2016
ISBN 13: 978-1-945761-02-7, ISBN 10: 1-945761-02-4
2009 Golden Crown Literary Society Award - Speculative
Fiction

In A Family Way – Book One of the Commitment Series
First edition published by Blue Feather Books, March, 2010
Second edition published by Badger Bliss Books, Sept, 2014
Third edition published by Badger Bliss Books, August, 2016
ISBN 13: 978-1-945761-05-8, ISBN 10: 1-945761-05-9

Unchained Memories – Book Two of the Commitment Series
First edition published by Blue Feather Books, Oct, 2011
Second edition published by Badger Bliss Books, Sept, 2014
Third edition published by Badger Bliss Books, August, 2016
ISBN 13: 978-1-945761-06-5, ISBN 10: 1-945761-06-7

Happy Campers - Book Three of the Commitment Series
First edition published by Blue Feather Books, Sept, 2013
Second edition published by Badger Bliss Books, Sept, 2014
Third edition published by Badger Bliss Books, August, 2016
ISBN 13: 978-1-945761-07-2, ISBN 10: 1-945761-07-5

The Blue Feather
First edition published by Blue Feather Books, July, 2014
Second edition published by Badger Bliss Books, Sept, 2014
Third edition published by Badger Bliss Books, August, 2016
ISBN 13: 978-1-945761-04-1, ISBN 10: 1-945761-04-0

Collective Identity – Book Four of the Commitment Series
First edition published by Badger Bliss Books, January, 2015
Second edition published by Badger Bliss Books, August, 2016
ISBN 13: 978-1-945761-08-9, ISBN 10: 1-945761-08-3

All My Tomorrows – Sequel to Yesterday Once More
First edition published by Badger Bliss Books, May, 2015
Second edition published by Badger Bliss Books, August, 2016
ISBN 13: 978-1-945761-03-4, ISBN 10: 1-945761-03-2

Sweet Angel – Book Five of the Commitment Series
First edition published by Badger Bliss Books, June, 2015
Second edition published by Badger Bliss Books, August, 2016
ISBN 13: 978-1-945761-09-6, ISBN 10: 1-945-761-09-1

Relative-ly Speaking – Book Six of the Commitment Series
First edition published by Badger Bliss Books, March, 2016
Second edition published by Badger Bliss Books, August, 2016
ISBN 13: 978-1-945761-10-2, ISBN 10: 1-945-761-10-5

1140 Rue Royale
First edition published by Badger Bliss Books, Sept, 2016
ISBN 13: 978-1-945761-00-3, ISBN 10: 1-945761-00-8
2017 Golden Crown Literary Society Award – Paranormal
Fiction

Tailspin- Book Seven of the Commitment Series
First edition published by Badger Bliss Books, December, 2017
ISBN 13: 978-1-945761-22-5, ISBN 10: 1-945761-22-9

Flashpoint – Book Eight of the Commitment Series
First edition published by Badger Bliss Books, December, 2018
ISBN 13: 978-1-945761-24-9, ISBN 10: 1-945761-24-5

Over The Crescent Moon
First edition published by Badger Bliss Books, June, 2019
ISBN 13: 978-1-945761-26-3, ISBN 10: 1-945761-24-5

COMING SOON FROM KAREN D. BADGER AND BADGER BLISS BOOKS

www.badgerblissbooks.com

In The Blink of an Eye - Book IX of the Billie/Cat Commitment Series
- Series
- Tentative release, year-end, 2019

Love In The Shadows
- Paranormal
- Tentative release, 1H 2020

Udder Nonsense - Book X of the Billie/Cat Commitment Series
- Comedy
- Tentative release, year-end, 2020